MALEVOLENT

A HIP-HOP LOVE TRIANGLE

ALEXIS SOLEIL

ISBN 979-8-9946035-1-2

CONTENTS

PLAYLIST

"MASS APPEAL" - Gang Starr
"DO YOU BELIEVE"–The Beatnuts
"HONEYMOON FADES" – Sabrina Carpenter
"THE EMPEROOR'S CURSE" – Wu Tang Clan and Redman
"ALEJANDRO" - Lady Gaga
"GIVING YOU THE BEST THAT I GOT" - Anita Baker
"YEAR OF THE CAT" - Al Stewart
"YOU BELONG TO ME" - Doobie Brothers
"ON AND ON" - They
"WHAT A FOOL BELIEVES" - Doobie Brothers
"INTRO (The First Step) - Gang Starr
"SUGAR" - Maroon Five
"YOU SANG TO ME" - Marc Anthony
"GLASS CEILING" - Matilda Mann
"SHOOT THE MOON" - Patti Austin
"FLOWERS" - J Dilla
"THE LOVE MOMENTS "- MagiCXbeats
"LOST STORY" - MagiCXbeats
"WAR AND DRUGS"- MagiCXbeats
"WELCOME IN" – MagiCXbeats
"LOVE IS GONNA GET YOU"- Krs-One
"BUTTERFLY BOOK" (Purple version) - MagiCXbeats
"SOMETIMES" – Noreaga
"100%" – Big Pun featuring Tony Sunshine
"IT'S SO HARD" – Big Pun featuring Donell Jones
"STILL NOT A PLAYER" – Big Pun featuring Joe
"TWINZ" – (Deep Cover 98) - Big Pun featuring Fat Joe
"LEAN BACK" - Terror Squad featuring Fat Joe

"FLOWERS FOR THE DEAD" - Cuban Link (RIP Big Pun)
“HERE COMES A FEELING” - Louis the child, Naomi Wild, & Couros
"OFF THE BOOKS" – The Beatnuts featuring Big Pun, Cuban Link
"DA ROCKWILDER" - Method man and Redman
“PAPER THIN” – MC Lyte
"NEXT LEVEL"- Showbiz and AG
"SOUL CLAP" - Showbiz and AG
"TRIUMPH" – Wu Tang Clan
"C.R.E.A.M." – Wu Tang Clan
"REIGN OF THE TEC" – The Beatnuts
“STOP, LOOK, AND LISTEN” – MC Lyte
“THE GIRL IS MINE” – Michael Jackson and Paul McCartney
“BAILAMOS” – Enrique Iglesias
“DANCE THE NIGHT” – Dua Lipa
“PARADISE DIMENSION” – MagicXBeats
“SOY UN GANGSTA” – Nore featuring Tru Life, Big Mato
“PURPLE PARADOX” – Adult Swim Bump
“SONG CRY FREESTYLE” – Tru Life
“JOHN BLAZE” – Fat Joe featuring Nas, Big Pun, Raekwon, and Jadakiss
“HEATWAVES” – Glass Animals

CHAPTER ONE

The soundproof walls of a darkened recording booth and a pop-filtered vintage microphone created a sealed environment for achieving the perfect musical sound. Adjacent to it was an enormous music studio with a sizable glass window showcasing a grand black piano, guitars, a bass, a drum kit, percussion instruments, microphones, and additional equipment in the background. A boom-bap baseline pulsed in the ears of handsome, medium-built Alejandro Valasquez, also known as MC Malevolent, age twenty-nine, who nodded along to the track as he rapped. He sported a black long-sleeved t-shirt with a fashion brand, black jeans, sneakers, a gold chain with a machete pendant, and a short, neat haircut. His best friend and business partner, Lorenzo Porter, also known as DJ Loco, bobbed his head to the music while sitting behind the soundboard. Benji, Lorenzo's manager, and two studio techs were also present. Behind them sat Loco's somewhat of a girlfriend, Jazzy, along with a few more groupies and neighborhood tagalongs from Rego Park, Queens. A young female receptionist stood in the doorway with paperwork in her arms, unable to resist listening to the handsome Latino guy rapping. Her presence went unnoticed as everyone was captivated by Malevolent's talents. Whenever he was in the studio, the vibe was always electrifying.

"I'm Malevolent
Heard that they ain't ready yet
Leave the scene a fuckin' mess
Aiming at your fuckin' head
These bars like a knife
Like a stick like machete
I aim it at your head
Heard nobody ain't ready
Ready
See I'm Malevolent
These rappers up against
Somebody they ain't never seen
Like in the fuckin' flesh,
I leave the scene a mess
Y'all rapping' wit the best
Each time I battle rap like 8 mile
Straight for your heads
These bars they love the blood
Machete wit the cuts
The lava wit the flow
Some vodka on the rocks
The bar's hitting got a bite
Make your stomach drop, drop, drop, drop
I'm Malevolent
Heard that they ain't ready yet
Leave the scene a fuckin' mess

Aiming at your fucking head
These bars like a knife
Like a stick like machete
I aim it at your head
Heard nobody ain't ready
Ready,"

Malevolent rapped with passion, enjoying the crowd's response to his style. As the music played, Loco moved his body, listening to the lyrics from his best friend, and gave him a thumbs up. As a hip-hop duo, Loco focused on creating beats and crafting their brand identity, requiring a unique name to captivate listeners everywhere.

"I'm Freddie Kruger in the night
13th Friday
So the beat vibey
No MC can beat
How I keep rhyming
Been thru it all
And I'm still here climbing
Lost my Pops
Heard the shot
Wit the words that I spit
It's a gotta price
If you are going up against
Me, the best, most definitely
Lift these rappers off my back
Like I'm reppin'it
I'm Malevolent
Heard that they ain't ready yet
Leave the scene a fuckin' mess

Aiming for your fuckin' head
These bars like a knife
Like a stick like Machete
I aim it at your fuckin' head
Heard nobody ain't ready
Ready!
Yo! Shout out to my main man, DJ Loco! My peeps in
Corona, East Elmhurst, Lefrak, Jackson Heights, Woodside, Astoria, Queensbridge, South Jamaica, Hollis, Queens Village,
all on Strong Island, The boogie down Bronx, Brooklyn, my peeps uptown, downtown, and all around to the Garden State and the rest of my fans. Much love. And to my Pops, Edgar Luis Velásquez. I miss you.

Malevolent said, *"Love you,"* as he removed his headphones. A smirk crossed his face after completing the task. With applause from Loco and the entire recording studio, Malevolent pushed open the booth door, celebrating the success of their new track.

Minutes later, the rhythm took hold, and soon Malevolent and the group were nodding along to the track. Loco and Malevolent bumped fists in celebration. The studio engineer at the soundboard experimented with controls to get the best audio. Malevolent stopped swaying with the music, his face flushing red as he punched the sound engineer.

"What the fuck are you doing? Why are you fuckin' with the sound?" Malevolent demanded, suddenly stood from the recliner.

"Mal, relax! He's trying to figure out a great sound!" Loco tried to calm his friend down.

"My apologies!" the sound engineer pleaded. Loco bumped fists with Malevolent as he sank back into his recliner. Loco emphasized the financial investment in studio time, reminding Malevolent of their goal to release an entire album, not just singles. Shaking his head, Malevolent apologized for his boisterous behavior as Loco proceeded to discuss their ambitions out loud.

To soothe his best friend's tensions, Loco introduced Jazzy, a beautiful, hourglass-figure woman with emerald eyes also from Rego Park. Struck by her beauty, Malevolent understood that this was Loco's lady. But his eyes widened as he beheld the enormity of her large buttocks. To his surprise, Jazzy's rear end repulsed him. "What did she hope to achieve by investing in butt enhancement surgery?" he wondered.

Malevolent stood from his chair, shook her hand, and conversed about his gifts and destined greatness. While his words flowed, this Jessica Rabbit-type woman stroked his chest and held the machete charm in her palm. He could tell that she didn't seem interested in his music; she was just after the money. As Jazzy gushed over Malevolent's fancy jewelry, Loco leered at her ample backside. Malevolent fabricated an excuse to distance himself from her and hurried out of the studio. Lorenzo's face lit up with a devilish grin as he slapped Jazzy on the behind. She threw her arms around him.

Ignoring his surroundings, Malevolent sprinted past the studio's dimly lit lobby's front desk in under a few seconds. The mahogany-toned, African-American young woman, early twenties, stroked the keys of the brightly lit computer under a side lamp. Malevolent caught a glimpse of this diligent woman, who appeared entranced by her work. She remained steadfast on the screen, oblivious to the eyes on her.

"Hello!" Malevolent greeted, revealing himself.

She sprang up from her chair, holding her hand on her chest as her breaths quickened.

Malevolent apologized for scaring her. The office lacked sufficient lighting, so he attempted to find a light switch. More light appeared, and upon seeing her beautiful face, he apologized again to the hardworking young woman. He introduced himself, shook her hand, and smiled. She then mirrored his smile as they became better acquainted.

“I’m Portia,” she introduced herself.

She had knowledge of Malevolent's abilities, ambitions, and talents from the recording booth and office receipts she came across. His impressive music, with a ninety-style sound, would reach all ears, globally.

"Are you feeling, okay?" With a firm grasp, Malevolent held her hand, fearing she might tumble over.

"I'm fine," Portia replied, catching her breath.

With her full attention on the hip-hop star, Portia asked, "Is there anything I can do for you, sir?"

His head hung low as a snicker escaped his lips. "Sir" made him feel uneasy, as if he were old.

"Sir?" His snicker deepened, a playful tone in his voice.

"Mr. Valasquez, I'm sorry for my oversight," Portia said.

"Call me Mal," he suggested.

"Malevolent?" Portia asked, questioning whether her actions had conveyed the proper level of respect.

"Yes, Malevolent," he smirked, pressing a kiss to her hand, longing to learn more about her. Portia emitted an introverted vibe while Malevolent made his extroverted, flirtatious actions known. He found fascination in a woman who spoke very little, which shrouded her in mystery. Malevolent recalled a girl in high school who was quiet and enigmatic. He hoped to get to know her but learned she had switched schools.

"I noticed you just started working here," Malevolent said

while scratching his eyebrow. "You're awfully quiet. Where did you go to school?"

"Do you mean college?" Portia tapped a pen on her desk.

"College or high school. Wherever," he replied.

"I attended the University of Oxford in London," Portia said with a smirk.

"Oh, London. Is it really cold and dreary?" Malevolent asked.

"Sometimes. And there are sunny days," Portia replied. She then inquired about Malevolent's life. "I attended Queens College and got my bachelor's. I'm a night crew manager at the supermarket," Malevolent sighed. She checked the clock, noticing it was ten-thirty-four, then powered off the computer and straightened up the desk.

Malevolent observed as Portia retrieved her coat from the rack. "Do you have a man?" he asked as she hurried to leave.

"No. I'm single," Portia replied as she slipped on her jacket, throwing her handbag onto her shoulder and rushing out of the studio.

"What's your hurry, baby?" Malevolent called after her, making an effort to become familiar with her.

Outside of the recording studio, minutes later, a green taxi halted at the curb. Malevolent opened the rear passenger-side door for her as she got in.

"I'm sorry to be so abrupt," Portia said.

"I'll see you tomorrow," Malevolent said, slamming the taxi door shut.

"Let's continue this conversation tomorrow. And I can hear some of your music," Portia smiled. A spark of attraction lingered in their shared gaze. Malevolent yearned for the following day to deepen their bond. He only knew that Portia was beautiful. Perhaps this could be beneficial for both of them. Malevolent approached the driver's side, handing the taxi driver a fifty-dollar bill for Portia's ride home. He winked at her as he stepped away from the cab.

"Get home safe, beautiful," Malevolent said as the taxi drove off. As she looked out the back window, he waved. He kept his cool to avoid jeopardizing his opportunity, especially if she wasn't interested in dating a rapper. He swaggered back into the studio to complete his recordings.

CHAPTER TWO

The screeching brakes of a gray Dodge Challenger pulled into the recording studio parking lot as rap music played at a reasonable volume within the vehicle. Malevolent halted the car's engine just as the music finished. Jumping out of the driver's seat, he slammed the door shut and hurried toward the recording studio. Three security guards kept an eye on the premises to ensure everything was secure. Upon recognizing this future hip-hop star, their lack of authority made it clear that these guys on the job were starstruck. With anticipation for Malevolent's music, music videos, and shows, they bumped fists with him.

Malevolent was in the dark about his future. He wasn't in a rush, taking things as they came, and he hoped to reach his destination without letting his success inflate his ego. Rushing through the heavy door, he dashed down the narrow hallway. He could hear a piano playing and felt as if he just entered Carnegie Hall. "Who is playing *"The Flight of the Bumblebee?"* he wondered. The pianist displayed skill as the high-pitched sound of the keys rang in his ears.

He breezed past the front desk, noticing that no one occupied the recliner. A tropical wallpaper was displayed on the computer screen, and luckily there were no phone calls coming in. With a confident swagger, he entered the recording studio as the piano became even louder, the instrument's vibration hammering through his body. He noticed Loco's entourage and groupies, as well as studio employees, who were watching the pianist's fingers maneuver along the keys of a magnificent black Steinway piano. Malevolent weaved his way through the crowd and approached Loco's side.

"Mal, check this out," Loco nudged him. Malevolent's eyes widened, recognizing the woman he had startled the night before—Portia—mastering the piano. Her talents were worthy of Carnegie Hall, and she had great potential to perform there. He smiled, revealing her to be more than just a pretty face; she possessed the abilities necessary to achieve greatness. He pondered which musicians she held in high esteem. Was it Mozart or Beethoven? Was she into jazz, classical, or pop music? Did she have aspirations to perform? At what age did she start playing, and how long had she been at it? He was determined to find out over dinner.

Portia's piano performance ended with a burst of applause from her admirers. Malevolent moved towards her, swaggering in astonishment. He wrapped Portia in a tight embrace and said, "Wow!" He desired to kiss her but thought it was moving too fast. He was petrified of driving her away and embarrassing himself. Portia didn't seem bothered by his embrace as their gazes locked.

Loco abruptly kissed her on the cheek. Malevolent held back his frustration as his friend and business partner appeared poised to get in her space. Yet Portia's musical talents captivated Loco as well. "Would you be interested in collaborating with Malevolent on some music?"

Malevolent gazed into her eyes to gauge her response to the offer. Portia reciprocated the gaze of this next rap legend.

"Yes, that'll be great," Portia replied, smiling at Malevolent and shrugging her shoulders.

"Portia and I will discuss it over lunch. Is that cool with you, Portia?" Malevolent smirked, gazing directly into her eyes.

"Yes, it's cool," Portia shrugged again.

Elevator music played from the ceiling of a Queens diner that afternoon as Portia and Malevolent settled into a booth. They were quiet, sharing only a romantic gaze as Portia observed the tiny fairy lights adorning the artificial plants, old-world paintings, wall décor, and photos of famous people who had dined there, along with servers bustling to serve meals. Malevolent noticed she grimaced a lot and was a big dreamer. But with her gift, Portia’s dreams would become a reality. She set her eyes back on Malevolent.

"What made you choose the name Malevolent?" Portia asked with a touch of shyness.

"My past has some baggage that I'm not ready to unpack right now," Malevolent exhaled.

"So, what's your actual name?" she asked.

"Alejandro Valasquez," Malevolent smirked.

"That's beautiful," Portia remarked, smiling while averting her gaze. Her mahogany complexion displayed her red undertones, making her beautiful, and gave off a glow that made Malevolent smile.

"Portia, why did your parents give you that name?" Malevolent asked. "No, let me guess: because your parents wanted a Porsche. As an alternative, you were named after a luxury sports car," he chuckled.

Portia nodded, confirming Malevolent's guess. “My mother wanted a cherry red Porsche, but the price tag was too steep. And so, here I am—Portia!" she giggled.

Malevolent and Portia shared a laugh as a young server placed two glasses on the table and filled them with water. He then placed two menus in front of them.

"Thank you," Portia said with a smile.

"Are you ready to order now?" the server inquired.

"Give us a minute, please," Malevolent answered.

"Call me when you're ready," the server strutted away.

Leering at Portia, Malevolent placed his menu down on the table. He felt an urge to convey something significant to her. He kept a cool facade even though he was doing something somewhat rude. The hug he had given her felt inappropriate. Curiosity sparked in Malevolent as he wondered if it had made her uncomfortable. Time would tell the outcome.

While pretending to be absorbed in the menu, Portia couldn't ignore the handsome guy who wouldn't stop staring at her. She sought refuge behind the large menu.

"Talk to me babe," Malevolent grabbed the menu from her hand.

"Tell me about the music that's influenced you," she whispered.

"Hip-hop artists from the '90s—are you familiar with hip-hop music from that time?" Malevolent asked.

"Indeed, I am. It was the perfect time for that," Portia said.

"And the early 2000s. Do you enjoy rappers like Capone and Noreaga, Brand Nubians, Fat Joe, Cuban Link, and Showbiz and AG?" Malevolent asked. "Do you enjoy listening to jazz?"

"Not particularly. Classical and symphonic music are my thing," Portia remarked, taking a sip from her glass.

"Who are your all-time favorite composers?" Malevolent wanted to know.

"John Williams, James Horner, Danny Elfman, and I lean more toward house music—artists like Larry Heard and Kerri

Chandler, famous for their keyboard and synthesizer sounds. Learning to use synthesizers for music has always been a dream of mine," Portia said.

"That's cool." Malevolent took a sip of his water.

"Ready to order?" the server asked, holding a digital menu.

Queens Boulevard was Malevolent and Portia's path, leading them toward the recording studio. There was a silence between them as they kept their eyes fixed on one another. By the romantic stare in their eyes, both wanted to go further but felt the need to take it slow. Malevolent swaggered closely to Portia, noticing her walking on the outside of the sidewalk while he was on the inside. He gently grabbed her by the waist and placed her on the inside of the sidewalk while he swaggered on the outside. Portia's eyes widened at his sudden move. Still, no words were exchanged; they continued their shared gaze. Malevolent could tell by the look in her eyes that she felt safe. He returned the smile, letting her know that it was okay.

The noise of trucks driving along the four-lane boulevard would drown out their conversation even if Malevolent asked about her past relationships and the characteristics she sought in a significant other. He still wouldn't be able to comprehend what she conveyed. They needed more time together alone in a quiet place. He hoped she wanted a man with success, good looks, and a good heart. *That's what every woman wants, right? Maybe not. Probably not a rapper. Portia would likely marry a doctor or a stockbroker while making a name for herself.* Malevolent and Portia walked shoulder to shoulder as if they were going to lean in for a kiss but maintained their composure. His nose caught a whiff of the fragrance she wore. He wasn't a perfumist but he guessed there were notes of vanilla, amber, cherries, and some floral ingredients.

"Portia, let me ask you something," Malevolent said upon reaching the recording studio.

"What's up?" she smiled.

"Were you offended by my hug?" he inched his shoulder away from Portia, not wanting his actions to contradict his question.

"Not at all," Portia shook her head, unconcerned by the idea. Malevolent's mind churned with more thoughts. *Was it right for him to do it? Was it the right decision for him?* With passion, he kissed Portia on the lips. She didn't think twice about pushing him away. Malevolent and Portia embraced in a fervent kiss. Malevolent received his answer.

Screeching tires of a black Jaguar E-Pace stopped short at the curb with Jazzy in the passenger seat. She stared, dumb-founded, as Malevolent embraced Portia, a person she had considered insignificant.

"Mal!" Loco hopped from the driver's seat and slammed the door. He trotted to his business partner and friend, bumping fists with him. Portia's beauty entranced Loco, and he locked his gaze upon her for a second. Malevolent sensed a challenge right before his eyes and aimed to ensure Portia stayed close to him. He wanted to be careful not to seem controlling; it was as if Portia were a toy his best friend wanted to take from him.

Malevolent's peripheral vision glimpsed Jazzy's fiery red face, frowning with crossed arms as she leaned back in the passenger seat. She knew about Loco's flirtatious behavior with every woman he laid eyes on. The thing Jazzy loved and respected about Malevolent was that he was focused on his craft—educated and wasn't a skirt chaser. Of course, Malevolent knew groupies were a common occurrence in the music industry, but he strongly believed in monogamous relationships. On the contrary, Loco, like most men, realized that it was not possible. Surprisingly, he had no baby drama despite his risky behavior. Loco had flashy appearances due to his clothes, car, and residency. Like Malevolent, he wore black attire, showcasing their somber and sometimes menacing image.

"How are you, Portia?" Loco smiled.

She whispered, "I'm fine."

"Are you still keen on collaborating on tracks with Malevolent? It would be great if you added your piano skills to it." Loco scratched his head.

"Yes, I can do that," Portia giggled.

"Cool. Malevolent and I want to make sure—you know, Carnegie Hall may snatch you up. We don't want to miss this opportunity," Loco chuckled.

"Portia's talent is undeniable. She's destined to play there," Malevolent declared, kissing her forehead. A devilish grin spread across Loco's face as he gazed at Portia.

"You're brilliant, Portia!" Loco stated. "You know that!"

"Thanks," Portia said with a shrug.

With a wink, Loco presented his business card to Portia. Malevolent observed his producer and friend engaging in flirtatious behavior. His eyebrow arched, and his face contorted into a frown. Loco bumped Malevolent's fist as he swaggered toward his car. The Jaguar hurtled down the street with its screeching tires. *"Was Loco being friendly or a little too friendly?"* Malevolent wondered. He then dismissed the idea as he and Portia waltzed into the recording studio.

"The Charlie Brown Waltz" filled the air while Portia's fingers glided along the black and white piano keys that evening. On the stool next to her, Malevolent observed her skilled fingers mastering the instrument. He wondered if she could play any other melodies. *"Why even ask that?"* Portia's skills were so exceptional that she could outperform any professional pianist.

Minutes later, she performed the theme song for "The Entertainer." A chuckle escaped her as she navigated the keyboard, and Malevolent remained quiet, observing her amusement.

"Could you play something dark?" he scratched his neck.

Seconds later, she navigated her fingers along the ebony and ivory keys, performing the "Dracula" theme.

"It sounds better on an organ," Portia said with a giggle.

Next, she played the "Halloween" movie theme song.

"Wow, that's cool! You are something special! Play one of your favorite love songs," Malevolent requested, his gaze hardening as she came to a standstill. She seemed to ponder the matter, making him raise an eyebrow in curiosity.

Then she put her hands on the piano keys and started playing an '80s R&B love song. Portia played Luther Vandross's "If Only for One Night."

"Do you know this song, Malevolent?" she asked, wearing a huge smile that released a burst of laughter.

"No. Should I?" he shrugged his shoulders.

"Aren't you familiar with Luther Vandross's music?" she asked, continuing to play.

"Yes, I am. But, I'm an amateur," he admitted.

"Your skills are impressive," Portia noted, smiling.

Malevolent shifted beside her on the bench. He walked his two fingers along the keys towards her hands and clutched Portia's hand. His heart hammered, convinced this was the perfect moment to act. Their eyes locked, burning with desire, inching towards Portia, and leaning in for a passionate kiss. His hand moved upwards under her blouse, targeting her breast. Malevolent felt a surge of smug satisfaction at her desire. It was possible that this was her first time. Her family moved a lot, so she had no chance to have a relationship or make love, for that matter. He pressed on her nipple and toyed with it. Portia moaned softly, showing her pleasure. A mischievous grin spread across his face. Malevolent questioned whether this would be the right time to make love. *"Not right now,"* he thought. *"When the time is right."*

Standing way in the dark background, Loco watched his best friend and the girl he had discovered first engaging in a kiss. In an instant, Loco's heart raced in his chest as a scowl crossed his face. He longed to be with Portia, yet it was his best friend who had her. Loco viewed Jazzy as nothing but a living plastic doll with no goals, no dreams, and no substance. She was the embodiment of the music industry's baddies. Portia was perfection from the first glance. Loco contemplated the possibility of girlfriend swapping with Malevolent.

Loco inhaled, hiding behind the wall while listening to Portia's enticing moans. "Shit!" Loco whispered, surprised by the sexiness of it. Then he heard smooches, laughter, and the piano playing. He peered back at his best friend and Portia, engaging in their romantic moment. There was nothing sexual going between them. And Loco wasn't surprised because Malevolent was private and kept his business to himself. Loco took a deep breath and departed with a swaggering gait.

CHAPTER THREE

A couple of nights later, the murky recording studio housed Malevolent and Portia, sitting before the grand piano. Portia's fingers slowly danced over the keys, producing a dark-toned melody while Malevolent listened. He desired an ideal sound for his new track titled *"Boom! In the Night,"* detailing the events surrounding his father's death. *"Chances are, Portia might inquire about what transpired that dreadful night,"* the thought crossed Malevolent's mind. He couldn't bring himself to tell her what had happened—not yet. He hoped his father was in a good place and wouldn't have to worry about someone causing him any more pain.

When Malevolent was a kid, he used to pray to God for his father's salvation. He gave up on praying and figured his father was probably in a bad place. Malevolent didn't mean to think that way, but it was what it was. He came from a Catholic background but didn't bother to go to church.

While Malevolent didn't believe he was evil, he did participate in fistfights, swearing, and other actions that didn't align with God. Yet, he had no criminal record but according to God, all sin is equal, no matter the size. His family reserved Malevolent's birth name, Alejandro, for their use. While at the piano, Malevolent sensed Loco watching him and Portia as he rocked in a recliner behind the soundboard. Beside him sat two sound engineers, who aimed to produce a powerful, rhythmic bass sound. Portia enchanted Loco like never before, even though her relationship with Malevolent was still new. Loco never thought about pursuing someone else's woman, especially not his best friend's. He turned to his sound engineers to check out the sounds they had come up with, nodding his head in agreement. Loco then fixed his eyes on Portia and Malevolent collaborating so closely. He had to figure out a way to get Portia all to himself.

"One might wonder, what about Jazzy? What's the story with her?" The only reason Jazzy was interested in him was because of his money and the name he had made for himself. Women like Portia were few and far between. She was an exceptional gem—a difficult pearl to find in the depths of the sea, or perhaps that one-of-a-kind diamond.

An hour later, Portia played an eerie melody on the piano while Malevolent stood at the retro microphone, adding his rap lyrics to the mix, wearing headsets. Witnessing the musical collaboration, Loco nodded his head, loving the powerful bass, the genius piano, and the bone-chilling lyrics in the song.

"Boom! In the night, lights out, sleep tight, for me
as a kid,
did nothing but dream of heavenly sights. Angels
were by night,
the moment was sadistic, an unlive realistic, a
bullet to the head,
you were another static, to the self-harm, being
unloved, underappreciated, I hated, that bullet

took you away, or was it my mother's disloyalty
drove you mad....,"

Malevolent rapped into the microphone, feeling the bass and piano in his ears. He sensed Portia directly behind him—her mastery of the piano was his support. Yes, it was support because she was going to help him create this great album for the world to hear. He didn't want to scare her away because of his dark past. He still had a dark cloud hovering over his head that he couldn't get rid of. Malevolent proceeded with the track, refusing to open his eyes. He was glad Portia didn't see his face because he had turned his back on her. *He wondered what she thought of this obscure track.*

"Boom! In the night, there goes the shot.
Seen my pops, stretched out on the floor, can't
give you
More of this horrific scene, blood everywhere, seeing
the red
Gave me a scare
My heart pumped fast, my blood ran cold
Too much blood, too much pain, this shit for a
kid my age, drove me insane,
Too much blood, too much pain,
my mother unloving you drove you insane,

While Portia navigated her long fingers along the black and white keys of the grand piano, all sorts of thoughts crossed her mind. *"What happened to Malevolent?"* she wondered, keeping the melody of the track. Goosebumps surfaced on her arms as Malevolent got more graphic about that night. On top of that, Portia's eyes watered, causing her vision to become blurry. She hoped not to make a mistake on the keys. She blinked constantly to clear her vision as the tears streamed down her face. Trying to keep her composure, Portia held back further tears. *"His mother?"* Portia wondered as she glanced at Malevolent, who continued the track with his back still to her. She couldn't wait for this session to end. With all the grief he had been through, the session felt infinite.

"Boom! In the night, there goes the shot,
raced down the hallway,
seen my pops shot, my heart cold,
blood everywhere gave me a scare,
my mother didn't care,"

Behind the soundboard, while Loco listened to his best friend's painful childhood, Jazzy crept up behind him, feeding him a green grape. She laid a kiss upon his cheek, placing herself in the chair by his side. Loco kept his focus on Malevolent's performance and on Portia playing the piano. Her playing those keys was so angelic that he noticed her tears from a distance. Loco didn't react to Jazzy's romantic gesture because it was obvious he wasn't in love with her. As Portia's fingers remained in tune with Malevolent's tragic story, the sound captured Loco's heart. Not due to his best friend's horrific experience, but because Loco also had a story of his own. He brushed his situation aside and knew Malevolent lived with his grandparents. He also knew little about Malevolent's father's death, which was something he preferred not to discuss. Now, because of this song that was about to go mainstream, everyone would know what had occurred that night. Jazzy then fed Loco another grape as he slapped the fruit out of her hand.

"Stop!"

"What's your problem?" Jazzy stood from her seat, shrugging.

"Don't you see I'm in a session now? Get out!" Loco pointed toward the exit.

Jazzy stormed out of the studio without picking up the fallen fruit. Loco kept his focus on finishing this track.

Minutes later, Malevolent concluded the song, his voice echoing out as he snatched his headsets off his head. He abruptly turned to Portia, noticing tears streaming down her face.

"Boom! In the Night!" touched her as she wiped her tears. She stood up from the piano, removing her headsets. The lovers shared tears while embracing one another. In the dark background, Loco watched Malevolent and Portia silently, not even saying a word over the speaker to congratulate them on a job well done or applauding as he usually did. He rocked in his recliner, teary-eyed as well. He immediately wiped them away, continuing to observe Malevolent and Portia stormed out of the recording studio, clutching hands. Loco had no reaction; it was as if they forgot they were even in a music session. And there was money on the line here. Luckily, this recording went well. Loco placed his fingers on the soundboard, lowering the volume of the recording.

CHAPTER FOUR

That Sunday morning, Malevolent navigated his muscle car through the streets of Douglaston, Queens, with its manicured lawns, stunning trees, and upscale homes. He nodded to the bellowing rap music from his radio, arching an eyebrow at this neighborhood that reminded him of something he had seen on television as a kid. He dreamt of living in a beautiful house of his own, confident that he was heading in the right direction. Admiring the fancy homes majestically perched on the hills, he gasped at the pleasantness of the properties. He decreased the music's volume, realizing he wasn't in the hood. "God, what a beautiful place," Malevolent muttered, proceeding to drive his Dodge Challenger along the smooth, paved streets. As he maneuvered his vehicle along a curved road, the waterfront homes captured his eyes. They widened as he saw more attractive houses and imagined Portia's stunning home. "You've reached your destination," his virtual navigator announced.

His imagination was right; an enormous blue and white Victorian waterfront home with a pristine lawn, trees, and peaceful nature settings welcomed anyone who entered the residence. The bright headlights of the muscle car parked as the engine shut down. Malevolent exited the vehicle, closing the driver's side door and he trotted up the small steps to the front door. Metal chimes blew in the wind right over Malevolent's shoulder as the sound rang in his ears. He rang the doorbell, which emitted a creepy sound, evoking a sign of death that he didn't like. Through the glass front door, Portia dashed downstairs, flinging the heavy door open. Portia and Malevolent wrapped into each other's arms and locked lips like reunited lovers. With a pot and dishtowel, Portia's mother, Mrs. Fairchild, a middle-aged woman, resembling the *"Clair Huxatable"* type, snuck up behind them. "Will you introduce me to your new friend, Portia?" Mrs. Fairchild asked, drying the pot.

"Oh, Mom! This is Malevolent. Well, Alejandro," Portia escorted him to her mother.

"You're the famous rapper!" a handshake transpired between Mrs. Fairchild and Malevolent.

"I'm working on it," he said modestly, scratching his eyebrow.

An African-American robust veteran, a six-foot-two gentleman, late fifties, observed this young man who had captivated his daughter's heart. Clearing his throat, he marched into their presence like a military drill sergeant, bringing Portia and Malevolent to attention. The two men confronted each other, poised for battle with direct eye contact. With a glare, they communicated their unspoken thoughts to each other.

"Was Portia's father in the military?" Malevolent wondered, sensing Mr. Fairchild's dominant and disciplined spirit, which would object to her being with a wannabe rapper. *"What type of future would they have?"* Mr. Fairchild asked himself. Neither man smiled, both being equally tall, and they shook hands. Malevolent wondered if Mr. Fairchild would tell him about life

in the military. He erased the thought and knew her father would interrogate him about his music. Mr. Fairchild abruptly snatched his hand away, marching back into the house without glancing back. Malevolent wasn't surprised by the sudden move; he snickered, shrugging his shoulders. He had nothing to hide; he wasn't a felon. He avoided misogyny and unnecessary violence in his lyrics. Portia and her mother witnessed the sudden, brisk nature of Mr. Fairchild's handshake. "Relax, Malevolent. He'll like you," Portia hugged him.

At dinner, Portia, Malevolent, and her parents gathered around the cherry wood table in the dining room, with a beautiful matching server visible behind them. Baby photos of Portia, along with school pictures from Scandinavia and other parts of Europe, adorned the walls. There were also images showcasing her piano studies throughout childhood, high school, and college years, along with pictures of Mr. Fairchild's military service in the Air Force, his medals, and more photos featuring Portia and her parents. A typical Sunday dinner comprised roast beef, potatoes, and vegetables for all. Malevolent felt at home, just like his family. Conversations meandered through everything going on in the world, and then Mr. Fairchild dove right into politics, entertainment, and social issues as they ate. Malevolent stayed quiet, giving the man the floor. Portia and her mother faced a similar situation, where their opinions were disregarded. Mr. Fairchild sipped his water before clearing his throat.

"Your political affiliation, Alejandro? Is it Democrat?"

"Neither party has my trust," Malevolent replied, swallowing his food and cleaning his mouth with his napkin.

"So, you're passionate about your craft?" Mr. Fairchild asked.

With a nod, Malevolent affirmed, "Yes, I am."

"What do your rap lyrics discuss?" Portia's father drilled him.

"The story of my life," Malevolent replied.

"Tell me about your life," Mr. Fairchild demanded, placing his glass down hard on the table.

The military giant and Malevolent engaged in a direct stare. He sensed Portia's nervousness in response to the rapid-fire questioning.

"My father blew his brains out when I was seven," Malevolent bluntly responded.

"Oh, Alejandro. Please accept my condolences," Mrs. Fairchild said, conveying her sympathy for the loss. She quickly consumed her water. Portia clasped Malevolent's hand, rubbing his back. Again, Portia's eyes watered.

"It was a pleasure meeting you, Mr. and Mrs. Fairchild. Thank you for dinner," Malevolent greeted the Air Force veteran with a handshake, then abruptly snatched his hand away. He exited the table in a huff, as Portia pursued him. Tears watered in Malevolent's eyes on his way to the car parked outside the waterfront Victorian home. Using his keychain, he unlocked his car door while feeling Portia sprinting behind him. He flung the driver's side door open, hopping into the seat while Portia hopped into the passenger seat as both doors shut. With an unwavering gaze, Malevolent didn't blink as a torrent of tears poured down his face. Simultaneously, tears streamed down Portia's face, and Malevolent caught a glimpse of it from the corner of his vision. He wiped her tears away as she did the same for him.

"My apologies," Portia's voice quivered.

"It's not your fault," he rubbed her cheeks.

"It's my father's fault. He's very strict and wants the best for me. I only know what's best for me," Portia gazed into his eyes as they shared a kiss.

"Boom! In the Night was about..." he shrugged his shoulders. Malevolent closed his eyes, attempting to fight back his fears. He opened them again, but the tears continued to flow down his cheeks. He hated for Portia to see him cry and didn't want to be a burden.

"I don't want to start off a relationship with issues. My issues," Malevolent inhaled, wiping his teary eyes.

"What's the issue?" Portia asked.

In a Catholic church in Corona, Queens, seven-year-old, black three-piece-suit-clad Alejandro and his entire family in black attire approached the house of worship on a dreary morning as its bells tolled. Young Alejandro held his grandparents' hands —Erasmo and Martha Valasquez, early fifties—as they clutched roses. He saw the rest of the family, some of whom he had never met, while others he knew very well. Alejandro's stunning aunts (Edgar's sisters), Tatiana and Deborah, slender-bodied with long black hair, were pillars of strength for their family in this time of need. Although Alejandro lacked uncles, he had many male cousins from his father and grandfather's side.

Alejandro realized how many people loved his father, seeing so many pay their respects. Tears flowed from every family member as they clutched roses, rosaries, and Bibles. Alejandro and his grandparents ascended the concrete steps of the church while he gazed at the roses in his grandmother's hand. He remembered that red roses are a Valentine's Day tradition—an occasion for happiness. *The roses grasped in her hand should've been black. Yellow roses existed, representing the state of Texas. Still a happy occa-*

sion. There should be black roses for sad days like this. Alejandro stepped into the religious foyer, crossing himself as tears cascaded down his cheeks. His grandfather consoled him, taking baby steps toward the black coffin resting before the altar. To avoid seeing his father, Alejandro shut his eyes. His father's suicide conjured an eerily personal horror film. In his grandfather's embrace, he rested his head against his chest. Crying and inching closer to the casket, he didn't dare peek at the corpse even once. His grandmother sobbed hard as Edgar embraced his wife and grandson. Erasmo's eyes watered as he sobbed, guiding Martha and Alejandro to the first bench with a clear view of the casket.

Alejandro's grandfather kissed and stroked his head. "Your father's in a better place now. We all loved him so much," Erasmo choked up, sobbing.

"Will I see him again?" Alejandro's voice quivered.

"Yes! You will see your father again," Erasmo assured him, shaking his head.

Alejandro lifted his head from his grandfather's chest, tears streaming down his cheeks. He wiped them away with his hands, sniffling. Edgar rested in a three-piece black suit on his way to a better place. Alejandro wondered about his father getting dressed up for an occasion like this—his death. Usually, people dress up for weddings or fancy parties, but this occasion was grief-stricken.

That afternoon, Alejandro and his family gathered at his grandparents' home in Rego Park to remember his father. Everyone shared pictures of Edgar from childhood to adulthood. There were also pictures of Alejandro with his parents, Edgar and his mother, Rosa. His Aunt Tatiana glared at a photo of her brother and Rosa together.

"Bitch!" she slammed the photo down on the coffee table.

She realized Alejandro witnessed her call his mother a derogatory name. Tatiana cradled her nephew in her arms, apologizing for her disrespect and kissed him on the cheek. Alejandro glared at his parents' photo, not crying or seeming angry while holding it in his hands. He ripped the photo in the middle, where his mother and father were. He placed his father Edgar's picture on the table and ripped his mother's picture. Tatiana sat on the sofa, shocked. She didn't know whether to stop her nephew from showing disrespect to his mother, regardless of the situation. But she allowed him to express his anger. There was an older gentleman who sat beside her, noticing Alejandro's behavior. He was shocked as well. Then Alejandro grabbed his parent's wedding photo and did the same with it. He ripped in the middle, then ripped his mother's photo into pieces.

"I hate her! This is her fault!" Alejandro sobbed, throwing his mother's torn picture on the floor. Tatiana rushed to comfort her nephew.

“It feels like it was yesterday when he died,” Malevolent held back his tears as much as he could. But he couldn't. “I've got some baggage,” he explained, wiping his eyes. He hoped Portia understood.

"Baby, everything's going to be fine. You've got your music, your life..." Portia encouraged him while holding his hand.

"And you," Malevolent smiled at her. They engaged in a passionate kiss.

Parked several feet away, Loco sat in the driver's seat of his black Jaguar E-pace, watching Malevolent and Portia from a distance. The lovers didn't notice the mysterious vehicle while they engaged in their loving kiss. Again, Loco watched a love story unfold and wondered how they were going to make it in this crazy music business. In Loco's mind, Portia seemed to be a girl who lived a fairytale and believed Malevolent was going to be her Knight and shining armor. Loco believed he could be that knight and shining armor. Now, he that was reality. Loco believed he would be a better fit for Portia. His name wasn't Loco for nothing. He peered through his rearview mirror, making sure there were no oncoming vehicles. He put the Jaguar in reverse, and sped off in the opposite direction with its screeching wheels.

CHAPTER FIVE

A glossy silver retro microphone perched on a stand in the darkened recording booth, waiting for words to give it life. A boom-bap beat bellowed from the speakers amidst the clamoring allure of women and the ruffian men in Loco's entourage. There was a spread of food on a long table, where anyone could grab a bite. Malevolent and Portia resided at the piano, trying to devise a tune for his next track. As usual, Malevolent sat close to her, focusing on his work and on her. He noticed Loco collaborating with studio engineers for another session. Malevolent eyed the piano's black and white keys again while Portia played. He turned beet-red in the face, pounded his fist on the keys, and sprang from his seat. "Get the fuck out of here! You motherfuckers are making too much mother fuckin' noise!" pointing to the exit. He startled the entourage as they lowered their voices, giving him the respect he demanded.

"I'm sorry, Mal," Loco rushed over to Malevolent, placing his hand on his shoulder.

"What the fuck, Loco! I'm trying to work here!" Malevolent shouted as he rushed back to the piano bench, kissing Portia on the cheek to let her know it was okay. She wanted to say something to him about the followers who wanted proximity to him, but that wasn't Portia's responsibility.

"We're spending money, Loco!" Malevolent reminded him. Loco turned his back on him, sucking his teeth. "I'm spending money. Shit, you owe money for these sessions," Loco mumbled under his breath. He clapped his hands to get the crowd's attention to inform them that there was an upcoming recording session.

In a smoky recording booth, Malevolent, wearing headsets, puffed on a marijuana joint while keeping his eyes wide open this time. He focused on Portia playing the ebony and ivory keys at the piano. She, too, wore headsets, hearing the boom–bap beat in her ears. Malevolent watched her mastering this magnificent instrument and smiled as he exhaled the smoky mist from his nostrils and mouth, stepping to the retro microphone.

"This is the Boom, Boom-Bap
This is the love for the Boom-Bap
This is the boom, boom-bap song
Can go wrong
Got this love so I rep it
Got this heart in my chest
And I rap to the Boom-Bap
Like nostalgic, we seek logic
MC Malevolent
DJ Loco
And the rest
Got my back
See these lines like a test

See these bars like a flex
In the gym
On the mic
Lift this weight off my back
I attack
I react
Like what's happening
When they come with the shots
With the bullets blasting,"

Malevolent spewed his words into the microphone. Loco and his entourage nodded along to the music. Loco then observed Portia working her fingers on the piano. He smiled, not only because Portia was so gifted; he gazed at her thighs spread apart while she played the notes of the black and white keys. Loco envisioned her lying on her back with her thighs wrapped around his waist, beads of sweat surfacing on their bodies between black satin bed sheets. He knew Malevolent and Portia just started seeing each other, but they weren't serious just yet. There were so many women in this music business who threw themselves at Loco, especially Jazzy. Malevolent and Portia had gotten together quickly, and hopefully, they would fizzle out just as fast.

"Up your mother fuckin' ass
See me bring in the cash
As I lash my words
To the boom-bap sound
I don't fuck around
So, you can boogie down
And groove
Make your body move
The Boom-Bap that bodies and ears approve

This is real
Authentic
Not synthetic
The Boom-Bap",

Malevolent continued with his great lyricism. He didn't allow anyone or anything to get in the way of his dream. He was ready to do his next track—whenever that would be. Minutes later, Loco, the studio engineers, and the crowd applauded Malevolent as he swaggered out of the booth. Loco was applauding and bumping fists with Malevolent. "That was dope!"

The noise-filled recording studio celebrated instead of preparing for another musical session, while Portia practiced on the piano. She noticed the entourage acting like buffoons while Malevolent and Loco stood face to face, chatting. Of course, Portia couldn't hear what they were saying, so she focused on her piano playing. She also noticed the very pretty women in the studio with their eyes glued on Malevolent. Portia wasn't an Instagram model or anything of the sort; she was an ordinary girl with musical skills. Inadequacies emerged in her mind, Malevolent was her first real boyfriend, and they had a lot in common. She didn't want to show that she was paranoid because it could turn him off or even worse, cause him to take advantage of her. She noticed Malevolent and Loco had sour expressions on their faces.

Portia turned away, thinking whatever those two were talking about couldn't be that serious or they would work it out. She attempted to play another tune but then pounded her fists on the piano keys. The clamoring of losers coming through the speakers from the recording studio broke her concentration.

"Malevolent! There's too much noise!" Portia whined, storming away from the piano and rushing to his side.

"I spent a lot of money here!" Loco waved his hands in the air.

"I know that! I'll pay you back, Loco!" Malevolent shot back.

"I don't mean to be heartless, but time is money and money is time!" Loco plopped into the recliner, rocking back and forth.

"The cash is coming," Malevolent turned his back.

"I'm trying to get this album completed," Loco stopped rocking in the recliner.

"No shit, Sherlock!" Malevolent hollered.

Malevolent and Loco glared at Portia for a second and then focused their eyes in the other direction. Both men noticed the entourage in the studio weren't aware of their spat. Malevolent sneered at these leeches who didn't do shit with themselves. He couldn't believe Loco entertained losers like this. Another BBL young woman similar to Jazzy, wrapped her arms around Loco, kissing him on the cheek. Loco squeezed her big juicy buttocks as she sat on his lap.

"Come on, baby. Let's go," Malevolent said as he and Portia exited the building.

Seconds later, the Dodge Challenger's headlights blinked, and the alarm chirped as Malevolent aimed his car keys at the vehicle. He held Portia's waist as they engaged in a passionate kiss. "I want you to spend the night with me," he said, kissing her on the cheek.

"Sounds romantic," Portia giggled.

"We could have lots of fun," he chuckled as they continued towards his car.

Just then, the heavy exit door of the studio swung open. "Malevolent!"

"What the fuck?" he mumbled.

"Where are you going, yo?" Loco trotted toward him.

"Wait in the car for me, Portia," Malevolent advised. Portia picked up her pace and hopped into the front passenger seat, slamming the door. She lounged in the seat, looking straight ahead.

"Where are you off to?" Loco waved his hands in the air again.

"It's getting late, man. I'm tired," Malevolent said.

"I get it. You're tired, alright..." Loco eyed Portia seated in the front of the SRT8.

“Not tonight, Loco!” Malevolent sighed.

“We've got more music to complete,” Loco pressed.

“Get rid of those fuckin' slacking-ass bums!” Malevolent raised his voice.

“They're not bothering anyone! Are they?” Loco arched an eyebrow.

“Yes, the fuck they are bothering me! And you're starting to bother me!” Malevolent got up in his best friend's face. Both men stood eye-to-eye, ready to hurl fists. Portia's eyes were glued to the glass window, hoping they weren't going to go to battle.

"They're bothering me! And Portia!" Malevolent's voice echoed.

“Get the fuck out of my face, Malevolent! Don't bite the hand that feeds you!” Loco yelled.

“I'll spit on the hand that feeds me!” Malevolent inhaled mucus, but spat on the concrete.

“You disrespect me, motherfucker! We've been down this road before!” Loco's voice boomed.

Malevolent hopped into the driver's seat of his Dodge Challenger and sped off.

During Malevolent and Portia's drive home, there was silence. The only sound was the SRT8 engine of his vehicle. Malevolent kept his eyes on the road, but he saw Portia from the corner of his vision. He sensed something troubled her because she was too quiet. It was probably the boisterous guys or the flirtatious groupies hanging in the studio. Portia didn't even look in his direction. Malevolent glanced at her while steering and focusing on the highway. "Portia, what's wrong? Why are you so quiet?"

He pressed his foot on the gas and picked up speed. Portia didn't respond. Malevolent's heart raced in his chest. "Portia! Answer me!"

"Those assholes!" she shouted.

"I know that, baby! How do you think I feel?" Malevolent lowered his voice.

"And..."

“And what?” Malevolent halted at a red light, refocusing his eyes from the road to Portia.

“You're going to be in the spotlight and you'll probably forget about me," Portia sank her body into the passenger seat.

"Fuck, no!" Malevolent revved the engine as the traffic light turned green.

He leaned toward Portia as they engaged in a kiss. Then the traffic light turned green while the lovers continued their passionate kiss. Horns honked from the vehicles behind them.

"Alright! Hold your fuckin’ horses!" Malevolent pressed down hard on the gas, speeding.

In no time, Malevolent parked his muscle car at the entrance of Portia's home, the brakes squealing with its monstrous engine. He shut down the vehicle and there was nothing but the sound of crickets chirping throughout the neighborhood. Malevolent and Portia eyed the stars in the night sky, lights out in the neighbors' homes along the street, and the occasional dog barking in the distance. Malevolent focused on Portia, caressing her hand and kissing it.

"We make beautiful music together, don't we?" Malevolent wrapped his arms around her waist.

"Yes, we do make beautiful music together," Portia replied, kissing him on the cheek.

"You're beautiful," he said, rubbing her cheek as they kissed.

Then the lights from the second-story bedroom window of the Fairchild home came on while a shadowy figure of a man stirred. Portia and Malevolent noticed they probably woke her father up, or he worried about her getting home late.

"My goodness. My father has probably been walking the floors all night," Portia shook her head as she and Malevolent watched the second-story bedroom window.

"He's worried about you being with me. I can't blame him," Malevolent said.

"There's no need for him to worry because we make beautiful music together," Portia chuckled.

"And you're beautiful," Malevolent pecked her on the cheek.

"We're beautiful," Portia pulled Malevolent closer as they kissed. Just then, her cell phone vibrated while she was still engaged in the kiss. She reached into her purse, searching for her phone as it continued to vibrate. She broke the kiss with Malevolent.

"Excuse me, sweetheart," Portia pressed the answer button on her cell. The caller ID read: Dad.

"Yes, Dad," Portia chuckled, noticing her father's shadowy

figure in the second-story bedroom window. Malevolent noticed the Air Force veteran's silhouette with his eyes fixed on his vehicle. He held Portia's hand, kissing her all over. Portia gently pushed him away because her father could hear the wet, noisy kisses.

"It's late, Portia," Mr. Fairchild said in a stern tone.

"I'll be up in a second, Dad," Portia replied before ending the call.

Portia and Malevolent engaged in their last kiss for the night. Malevolent began to kiss her neck, hoping to go further, but she gently pushed him away again.

"Baby, I've got to go," Portia sighed.

"I know. I want you to be there for me because I've got this album to complete. I need you, baby," Malevolent stroked her cheek.

"I told you. Yes, I'll be there, babe," Portia said, kissing him on the cheek. "Good night."

Portia exited the passenger side of the muscle car, closing the door. She blew a kiss to him as she walked to the front door of her home. Mr. Fairchild swung it open just as Malevolent watched Portia enter safely. He noticed the man of the house (Mr. Fairchild) slamming the door. Malevolent arched an eyebrow, shrugged, and sped away with his car's monstrous engine.

CHAPTER SIX

Raindrops poured against the windows of Malevolent's studio apartment in Rego Park, not too far from his grandparents' home. He rested his arm behind his head in his king-sized bed, deep in thought while wearing only boxers and his tattooed bare chest. He hoped that Portia could've spent the night with him. Malevolent stretched his arms and glanced over the ink design of a machete with his stage name on it, crafted in Times Roman font. He also did a once-over of his abdominal area where his birth name, "ALEJANDRO," was tattooed on his stomach. Then he looked at his shoulder, where a murky road with bare trees and a full moon was etched in black, blue, and red. He then focused on his lower arm, where a tattoo portrait of his father Edgar was engraved in black. The rich black ink made his father's image vibrant and beautiful. He shut his eyes momentarily, trying to sleep, when suddenly—BOOM! His eyes widened as he sat upright in bed, scanning his bedroom. It couldn't be gunfire; maybe one of the tenants upstairs was moving furniture or something had fallen on the floor. He glanced at the ceiling and strained to hear any more sounds.

Then there was quiet again, he punched his pillow and plopped his head back down. He shut his eyes again.

A silver moon loomed in the night sky over Flushing, Queens, New York. Young Malevolent (Alejandro), age seven, tossed and turned in his twin-sized bed in his small bedroom. Photos of him and his parents were pinned to the blue wall above his head. A small desk held some books and a handwritten letter to his mother that read:

Dear Mommy,

Do you still love me and dad. We miss you.

Please come home, so, we can be a family again.

Love Alejandro

He wanted to mail the letter to his mother the next morning. An overloaded toy chest rested in the corner, filled with all his favorite things. Alejandro's dingy sneakers were in the middle of the floor, and a Spider-Man nightlight gleamed throughout his small bedroom, providing comfort from things that went “Bump! In the Night.” He tossed in his bed and laid on his back, his eyes fixed on the ceiling. They shifted back and forth in his head, hearing his father in the master bedroom arguing. "I love you! Don't you understand that!" Alejandro's heart pounded, and he sat up in his slumber. His eyes scanned his bedroom, rushing to turn on the lights. He wished his father’s hollering would stop and knew he was on a call with his mother. This small boy heard his father's voice quiver. "You have a son! What about Alejandro!" Alejandro gasped, hearing his name and the sobs coming from the master bedroom. He crept to his bedroom door, cracked it open, and peered through. He saw his father striding down to the second floor with his cell phone to his ear.

"You'll be sorry! You'll be sorry when I'm gone," Edgar whined.

Young Alejandro emerged from his tiny bedroom into the hallway, leaning over the banister to hear more of his father's dreadful tears. He couldn't make out much more because all he could hear was sniffling and bubbly mucus. He sat at the top of the staircase, eavesdropping.

“You're going to make me do something crazy! You know that!” Edgar whined.

Alejandro didn't know why his father would do something crazy; whatever it was, he hoped it wouldn't cause any problems. Where did his mother and father go wrong? He wondered if he had something to do with their breakup. Maybe he should've gotten better grades in school or kept his room clean. Alejandro figured it was his fault.

“What does Claudio have that I don't?” Edgar's cry echoed from downstairs.

“Claudio? I hate him!” young Alejandro mouthed, raising an eyebrow. Just then, a glass crashed to the floor, and Edgar screamed, startling Alejandro. His heart raced, and his eyes brimmed with tears.

“I did everything for you, Rosa! And this is the thanks you give me!” Edgar darted from the kitchen throughout the house. Young Alejandro raced back to his room, easily shutting the door behind him. His father, Edgar, ascended to the second floor, continuing to sob. Alejandro could hear it all, like a giant monster invading their house. Yes, there was a monster who invaded their lives, and Claudio was that monster.

“You’ll be sorry when I’m gone, Rosa,” Edgar shouted.

“Going where?” young Alejandro mouthed.

"You can say goodbye to me, Rosa. And it's your fault that I must do this to my son," Edgar's voice echoed through the hallway.

“Goodbye!” Edgar hollered. Then—BOOM!

The loud bang startled young Alejandro, sending his heart racing. “Papi!” he cried, thrusting open his bedroom door and racing down the hallway to the master bedroom. He opened the door and gasped, seeing his father lying in a pool of blood. Edgar’s brain tissue and blood scattered on the floor, the nine-millimeter handgun still clutched in his palm. Young Alejandro fell to his knees and cried.

"You can’t be dead, Papi!" Alejandro sobbed, his heart shattering. Then he heard his mother’s voice on the phone.

“Edgar! Edgar! Answer me!” Rosa screamed.

Alejandro placed the cell to his ear. “Mommy, there’s blood everywhere! What did I do?” he cried.

“Oh my God! Edgar! I’m calling the police!” Rosa's voice muffled on the other end of the line.

"Mom! Mom, wake him up! Please!" Alejandro cried as tears cascaded down his face.

Back in the present, Malevolent’s tears cascaded down his face. He tossed and turned in his bed, his eyes snapping open. He scanned the room, realizing it was early morning and still dark. Sitting upright, he sobbed profusely. He hadn’t experienced these dreams about his father since he was thirteen, and they had stopped. For some strange reason, the nightmares were resurfacing, haunting him with horrible memories. He wished he had superpowers to prevent his father from taking his own life. Malevolent faced the reality that he was just a child—a small boy with limited strength.

An hour later, a light bulb from a floor lamp brightened above his head. With a pen and yellow lined paper in hand, he wrote more lyrical content to produce new music because this was his only superpower. He contemplated what title he would give his album. Would "Boom-Bap" be a successful single? Malevolent didn't want to get his hopes up too high. He sank into his lounge chair, listening to a hip-hop beat through his headphones. Hopefully, the beats would help him create something good, something genius, something that no one would ever forget. He held the yellow-lined notepad and pressed the pen to it, jotting down whatever came to mind.

"ROSES ARE BLACK,"
"Roses are Black,
mourners are blue,
I wished I would've wrestled that pistol from you,
Tears shed,
ashes to ashes,
dust to dust,
How can I trust,
When you went away,
How could I have convinced you to stay,
Roses are black,
mourners are blue,
I wish I would've wrestled that pistol from you,
Roses are black,
mourners are blue,
I wish I would've wrestled that pistol from you
Just a kid not knowing what I did,

I was good in school, not trying to be cool,
no fights,
no talking back, cause I would've got my fuckin'
face smacked,
my mother attacked your spirit,
your character,
and your heart,
Her torture tore you fuckin' apart,
then you met your demise,
tears shed,
ashes to ashes,
dust to dust,
how do I trust,
when you went away,
how could I have convinced you to stay,
Roses are black,
mourners are blue,
I wished I would've wrestled that pistol from you,
Roses are black,
mourners are blue,
I wished I would've wrestled that pistol from you,
Pops rest in peace,
love you,"

Malevolent put a period at the end of his song, placing his pen down and removing his headsets. He turned off the floor lamp.

CHAPTER SEVEN

"Lights! Camera! Action!" shouted a music video director as Malevolent stood before a silver retro microphone, spewing the lyrics to "Boom-Bap" into the shiny device. An Arriflex thirty-five-millimeter motion picture camera captured a close shot of him in the recording booth. The camera was positioned in the booth doorway, where Malevolent was in a cramped space. While he performed his song, Malevolent sensed the world staring right back at him through the camera's lens. Portia, Loco, the neighborhood entourage, studio engineers, and groupies— including Jazzy—nodded their heads to the beat, enjoying the show. Portia had a bright smile, watching Malevolent master his craft. She had some ideas in mind for the title of his album but decided to leave that up to Malevolent and Loco since it was their project—unless they asked for her input.

As the shoot proceeded, a masculine voice whispered in Portia's ear. "How are you, beautiful? You make my day every time I see you." She turned to find Loco, handsome at six-foot-two and close to two hundred pounds, glaring down into her eyes. He wore a long-sleeved black t-shirt with a sports logo, black baggy jeans, and construction boots, and the whiff of his cologne turned her on. Portia shook his hand, returning the friendly gesture and didn't sense anything out of the ordinary. But Jazzy, a few feet behind them, sipped soda from a plastic cup and noticed that Loco was a bit too friendly. She watched, grasping the cup tightly in her hand. Portia and Loco focused on Malevolent, who was getting closer to concluding the music track. Jazzy remained in the background, noticing Loco wrapping his arm around Portia's waist. Jazzy took the last gulp of her soda and crumpled the plastic cup in her palm.

"Malevolent is doing superb, isn't he?" Loco whispered in Portia's ear.

"Yes," Portia answered gently, feeling Loco's minty breath tickling her earlobe. She and Malevolent were about to become official, but Loco's powerful embrace sent shivers down her spine. She knew this wasn't a good look because this could make people think less of her. Portia cared about Malevolent and didn't want to do anything to hurt him, especially after he had endured such a traumatizing childhood.

"Are you coming to Flushing Meadows Park?" Loco asked with a smile that didn't seem threatening.

"Of course, I'll be there," Portia smiled in return.

"Anyway, I have to talk to Malevolent about completing this album. And you, sweetheart, can lay down more of your black and white keys on his tracks. How does that sound?" Loco asked.

"It sounds great. And I'll be at Flushing Meadows for his video," Portia shrugged her shoulders, nodding.

That night, the Unisphere in Flushing Meadows-Corona Park stood in the background of Malevolent's music video "The

Boom–Bap." At this second location, the film crew's bright lights lit the set while the Arriflex thirty-five-millimeter motion picture camera captured a wide angle of him rapping with friends, associates, and fans in the background. Mostly guys made up the crowd, with a few women present. Surprisingly, Portia remained behind the scenes, acting as if she were a production assistant. She watched Malevolent take the spotlight with Loco nodding to the beat alongside him. Just by seeing this hip-hop duo perform, any girl's panties would be wet. Malevolent and Loco sported their urban gear—black denim, long-sleeved black t-shirts with cannabis graphics, and boots. Thankfully, the warm weather offered them comfort as they paced back and forth under the steel globe looming overhead.

A beautiful young Latina college student named Marilyn offered Portia a bottled water. "Thank you," Portia said, taking the water from her hand and sipping the spring water. Marilyn was the script supervisor, cradling a clipboard with an AV script. The script was only about two pages long because there were only two locations.

“I wish I were in the company of two handsome rappers,” Marilyn giggled like a schoolgirl, gaping at Malevolent and Loco in the distance. She beckoned Portia closer to the camera so they could see the viewfinder of the music video in action.

“Look at how handsome they are! Just wait until this gets out to the world! Malevolent and Loco are going to be the hottest rappers!” Marilyn continued to giggle while Portia side-eyed this so-called college student.

“I admire your talent on the piano. How long have you been playing?” Marilyn asked, tapping her pen on the clipboard.

“I've been playing all my life. It's been years,” Portia answered, laughing a little.

“You’re the luckiest girl in the world to be collaborating with two soon-to-be hip-hop giants,” Marilyn lowered her voice so she wouldn’t distract the director’s focus.

“Lucky? I wouldn't call it that,” Portia snickered, shrugging her shoulders.

“My love life completely sucks, and I’m bored out of my mind if I’m not here on a production set. This keeps me motivated,” Marilyn said as her excitement dampened. Portia listened to this woman’s tales of failed romances and hopeful desires as if she were her therapist.

"How long have you been dating Malevolent?" Marilyn asked, her head cocked, eagerly waiting for an answer.

Portia lifted an eyebrow, wondering how she knew. "Not long," she shrugged her shoulders.

"Loco talks about you all the time," Marilyn added.

"He does?" Portia replied, surprised.

"Yes, Loco does. Like I said, you’ve got two handsome, successful men in your orbit. Aren't you the lucky one?" Marilyn turned her gaze back to Malevolent and Loco. Portia hoped this woman wasn't getting the wrong idea about her. Yes, she was seeing Malevolent, but why would it be luck that two guys were pursuing her? Portia wasn't even sure if Loco was interested in that way. Malevolent and Loco were business partners, best friends, and hopefully smart enough not to jeopardize their success over "little old her." She wasn't royalty or from a wealthy family; just a gifted pianist. But she didn’t want to appear too modest. “And why was Loco speaking about her to other people?” the thought crossed her mind. Loco could get her more opportunities in the entertainment industry. Then there was a roar of applause from the film crew for Malevolent and Loco, along with the crowd of onlookers in the video. Portia tapped her hand on the bottled water, her eyes catching Jazzy looking beautiful in her tight-fitting clothes that hugged her shapely body. Jazzy pressed her body close to Malevolent and kissed him on the cheek. Portia's heart raced as her eyes widened, witnessing Jazzy lean in to kiss Malevolent on the lips. She crumpled the plastic bottle in her hand and stormed off the set. But Malevolent turned his head before Jazzy could kiss him. He saw Portia walking off the set as a few photographers snapped photos of Malevolent and Jazzy. Malevolent had to smile for the camera and play it off. He gently pushed Jazzy away. "Come on! Get the fuck out of here, Jazzy!"

Loco grabbed her by the arm from behind. "What the fuck are you doing?"

"Nothing!" Jazzy wrestled out of Loco's grip.

"Well, it looked like something to me!" Loco responded.

The photographers continued capturing more pictures of Malevolent with other groupies and guys from the music video. So much attention showered Malevolent and Loco that even onlookers in the park shook hands with the Queens duo.

That night, doubt crossed Portia's mind as she lay in her full-sized bed, fairy lights hung around the frame illuminating her somewhat darkened bedroom. Tossing and turning in bed, she reached for her cell phone on the nightstand. The time read 2:32 a.m. She checked her call log and voicemail but found no calls from Malevolent. He hadn't even shown up at her home or sent her a text message. She attempted to dial his number but ultimately placed the phone back on the nightstand. Portia had yet to meet Malevolent's family, and she wondered if he would mistreat her or keep their relationship under wraps. She wanted to cry, but her spirit wouldn't allow her to shed any tears for a man who might years later land a role in a reality show as a washed-up artist. She turned her back toward the nightstand, trying to calm her racing thoughts.

CHAPTER EIGHT

Rap music blared throughout the recording studio the next morning, where Malevolent paced the floor with his cellphone to his ear. Loco and the studio engineers worked on the soundboard for another session. Besides the music playing, Loco's entourage and a few groupies horsed around.

"Come on, Portia. Baby, pick up," Malevolent murmured, exhaling with his cellphone pressed to his ear. He continued to hang on, hoping she'd answer his call.

"Come on," Malevolent grumbled, stomping his foot on the floor.

"Hello, this is Portia. Please leave your name and number, and I'll get back to you. Take care. BEEP."

"Portia! Baby, where are you? You've got me going crazy here!" Malevolent spoke in a stern tone, pacing the floor while Loco's clamoring friends bumped into him, causing him to drop his phone. "What the fuck! I can't hear myself talk or think!" his voice erupted through the studio. He raised his fists toward Loco's entourage, ready to throw a punch.

"My bad! My bad, Mal!" one of Loco's friends said, his

hands raised in the air. "Why the fuck are you motherfuckers in here?" Malevolent snatched his cellphone from the floor.

"Sorry, Mal!" another ruffian apologized. The group kept their voices down.

"Shit!" Malevolent swaggered into the larger music room, closing the door behind him. There was absolute silence in there, a peace as he settled at the piano. He took a deep breath, focusing on the black and white keys. "Portia, baby! It's not what you think or what you thought you saw. We've got to work on these tracks. Remember? I'll see you when I see you. And we'll talk," Malevolent ended his call. He fixed his gaze on the piano, wondering if she would believe him. From the corner of his eye, he saw Loco's entourage still horsing around while Loco rocked in his recliner. Malevolent wished Loco would get these losers out of the studio. He and Loco were businessmen, not clowns.

Loco glared at him as if he was trying to say something. The two men locked eyes in a menacing exchange that felt like a challenge. Malevolent couldn't figure it out; the visual standoff lasted less than a minute and left him feeling unsettled. Loco then retreated, continuing to collaborate with the studio engineers. Malevolent swaggered back into the studio, giving Loco's entourage the evil eye as they sat down and became quiet like children. Loco smirked at Malevolent, showing his dominance over these tagalongs. He stood from his recliner, bumping fists with Malevolent.

"What's up with Portia?" Loco asked.

"I don't know," Malevolent replied, dropping into the recliner across from Loco.

"She saw Jazzy trying to kiss me," Malevolent said, twirling in his seat.

"I apologize for that shit! I'm going to get on Jazzy for that!" Loco punched his fist into his palm.

“I need Portia on this album. I need her like a person needs air,” Malevolent said, stopping his twirling.

“Are you getting soft?” Loco cackled.

“No, I’m not soft. Why is it that when a man shows love to a woman, he’s soft?” Malevolent wondered, glaring at Loco. Loco continued to laugh it off.

“I didn’t think it was fuckin’ funny because I’m serious,” Malevolent said. It was almost love he felt for Portia, even though they were just seeing each other. As soon as Loco heard Malevolent’s words, his eyes widened in surprise. He didn’t respond but smiled, perhaps thinking it was too soon to love someone.

"Did you get the lyrics I sent you?” Malevolent asked.

"Yeah!" Loco nodded.

"I've got some more ideas," Malevolent said, scratching his eyebrow.

"What about?" Loco asked.

Malevolent folded his hands behind his head, stretching and rocking in the recliner. He glared at Loco for a second, staring straight ahead. "I want to title the album 'Mourning Rose,'" he replied.

"Mourning Rose? Roses in the morning? I don't get it," Loco leaned in.

"Mourning! Death and shit!" Malevolent rocked in the recliner.

"Alright, I get it. Something you and I have experienced," Loco nodded.

"Exactly! If Portia doesn't get here by eight o'clock, we’ll start without her," Malevolent threw his hands up. He turned his recliner to face the wall, where a clock hung. Malevolent stared at the long hand, the short hand, and the number eight. His eyes became heavier and heavier, as dozed off. “It's been a long day, from that video shoot to back in the recording studio," Malevolent muttered in his sleep.

"Alejandro! Alejandro, I see you're exhausted from your busy day," an unfamiliar voice spoke to him. Malevolent opened his eyes slowly, seeing a blurry figure standing before him. He wiped his eyes and gasped, staring at his father, Edgar. Edgar looked healthy, smiling, and without a scratch or bruise on his body. He wore a light blue sweater, jeans, and sneakers, with a heavenly glow about him. "God must've sent him down from heaven to check on me," the thought crossed Malevolent's mind.

"I came to tell you how proud I am of you. And I'm sorry for leaving you. Please don't allow anything to drive you to the edge. Whatever happens, just roll with the punches. Life has its difficulties. I love you. Take care, son," Edgar's voice echoed, accompanied by piano keys reverberating in the background.

Malevolent lifted his head and swung around in the recliner. He wiped his eyes, stood to his feet, and heard piano playing emerging from the other side of the studio. He couldn't afford to be tired, despite working the day before; he realized this was what it took to become successful in the music business. Long hours in the studio or long hours in any field—that's how a person's reached their dreams. Malevolent's heart raced, hoping Portia was at the piano. What if it was another pianist? If something happened to her, he would never forgive himself for not having Portia in the video with him. Next time, he promised himself, he'll have Portia right next to him.

"Portia!" Malevolent swaggered into the well-lit studio to find Portia at the Sterling grand piano. Her fingers danced along the black and white keys while Loco paced before the magnificent instrument on his cellphone. Malevolent stormed over to the piano, pounding his fist on the keys. He grabbed Portia's hands, demanding an answer. "You better have a good reason for leaving the set!" he tightened his grip on her wrists, anticipating that she would come up with some bullshit.

"Ouch! You're hurting me, Mal!" Portia wrestled her wrists from his grip.

"I want an answer! Now!" Malevolent pounded his fist on the piano keys again.

"You were busy. I didn't want to bother you!" Portia's voice quivered as tears trickled down her cheeks. Malevolent wiped one away, kissing her cheek.

"You're a part of my success. I wanted us to take pictures together, but you took off. You're my girl, remember!" Malevolent whispered.

"Of course, I acknowledge that!" she replied, taking hold of his hand, which was still balled into a fist. Portia noticed Malevolent's fiery red face and could tell he wanted to pound the piano keys like a punching bag. He eventually relaxed his hand, releasing his fist.

During this lover's quarrel, Loco stood to the side, glaring at Malevolent and Portia. He was holding his cellphone, clearly having finished his call and now enjoying a soap opera right before his eyes. He didn't bother to diffuse the situation. Malevolent and Portia sensed they were being watched, realizing Loco had stood there the entire time. "No one acts like that," Malevolent realized and sensing Loco's bizarre behavior.

"I just spoke to Joe Jose's manager, and I want you guys to collaborate on some tracks together. How does that sound?" Loco tittered.

"That's cool with me," Malevolent smiled back, playing along. He and Loco bumped fists and embraced, discussing more upcoming projects. "Joe Jose" was a Bronx rapper with international fame, having risen from the gritty sidewalks of Tremont. In addition to his music, he appeared in several Hollywood movies and made a cameo in a TV show. Malevolent had never met Joe but was an admirer of his style and accomplishments. Loco invited Joe to check out Malevolent in the studio to help them become more acquainted. Malevolent felt self-assured about his work, with Loco playing a secondary role in getting him to the big time.

Clacking black high heels echoed on the wooden floor of the studio as Jazzy wrapped her arm around Loco's waist, kissing him on the cheek. Immediately, Loco grabbed her by the wrist and escorted her out of the studio.

"What the fuck is your problem?" Loco hauled Jazzy out of the music instrument room like a rag doll.

"You're hurting me, Loco. Let go of me!" Jazzy screamed. Loco and Jazzy made their way out of the recording studio, past everyone, who witnessed the encounter in shock. "Holy shit!" one of Loco's friends shouted, eating ice cream.

"Get off me, Loco!" Jazzy raised her voice, clearly distressed.

Loco kicked open the heavy rear door leading to the parking lot. Jazzy attempted to wrestle her way out of Loco's grip, but he had a strong hold on her. She almost stumbled in her high-heeled shoes but regained her balance. "You're going to make me fall!" Loco shrugged, not uttering another word. He didn't care if she plummeted onto the concrete. He pinned her against the wall of the building, glaring into her eyes, then aggressively kissed her, lifting her skirt and attempting to tear her panties.

"What the hell are you doing?" Jazzy screamed.

"3-0-4!" Loco stepped back from Jazzy, eyeing her from head to toe.

"You're going to fuck me in public!" she screamed, tears welling in her eyes.

"It's not the first time," Loco shook his head. His entourage stood in the background, cheering him on and poking fun at Jazzy. "Why did you have to step into my life?"

"My DMs are full of men who want to be with me! I've got ballers! Rappers! Businessmen! I've got over a million followers!" Jazzy pointed in Loco's face.

"Do what you're good at—take off your clothes! 3-04!" Loco and his cronies cackled in unison as he swaggered back into the building, shutting the door behind him. Jazzy flipped him the finger while she stumbled down the street in her high heels.

Loco made his way down the small dark corridor to the recording studio, his entourage right behind him. Rap music continued to blast from the speakers while the studio engineers worked the soundboard. Loco's reflection appeared on the glass of the instrument room, where Portia and Malevolent remained at the Sterling piano, cuddling, holding hands, and kissing. Loco's thoughts turned dark. *"What about his love life?"*

CHAPTER NINE

That evening, Loco steered his black Jaguar through the neighborhood of Woodside, Queens, where he cherished memories of his past. The car's wheels screeched as he halted at a red traffic light. Loco's eyes watered as a tear trickled down his face; he quickly wiped it away. He couldn't stand the idea of getting emotional, but there was a good reason for it. He eyed a young couple holding hands, strolling on the sidewalk, and could tell they were in love. *"Your first love,"* Loco remembered it too well. Then the traffic light turned green, as he drove along the boulevard, steering his vehicle onto a residential block where some Reggaeton music played in the distance. He wondered if there was a block party or if some guys were just hanging out in the park. He had participated in block parties all over New York, meeting dozens of neighborhood residents and even movers and shakers in the music industry. Loco parked his vehicle in front of a house, where some neighbors sat on their porch, and conversing in Spanish. He exited the driver's seat, slamming the door, and dashed to the front door, ringing the doorbell. As he peered over his shoulder, he noticed the two Latina women on the porch.

"Hola!" Loco smiled and waved. The two women exchanged giggles. The sound of locks clicking echoed as a brunette woman, Mrs. Veico, mid-fifties, stepped forward to greet him. Placing her hand over her heart, she embraced him. "Lorenzo! How are you?"

"I can't complain," Loco replied, new tears forming in his eyes. "Can I see her?" he asked Mrs. Veico. Choked up by Loco's request, she nodded and widened the screen door as he entered the house.

Loco swaggered into the living room, scanning the typical setup: a couch, recliners, a coffee table, and family photos adorned the walls alongside paintings and other art. In one corner stood a fireplace, atop which rested a silver urn engraved with a violin symbol. Loco inched towards it, his tears dripping like a leaky faucet. The urn read: Zadie Veico, date of birth, and date of death. Zadie's gorgeous eight-by-ten photo displayed as she smiled from ear to ear, but it blurred in his eyes because of his tears. He sat in a recliner, closed his eyes, and could hear her sweet voice.

"Lorenzo! Lorenzo!"

On a not-so-crowded Queens college campus, students rushed to class, while others socialized and enjoying the nice spring weather. A younger-looking Lorenzo, dressed in baggy jeans and a long-sleeved t-shirt, looked in every direction, hearing his name. He smirked, scanning the enormous crowd until he spotted her—Zadie, a vibrant young woman who rushed into Lorenzo's arms, violin case in hand. They kissed as lovers do, oblivious to the crowd of students who paused to observe.

"How are you?" she asked, kissing Lorenzo's cheek.

"I'm cool," he replied, smiling. "I see you're cool."

"Yes, I am. I missed you," Zadie said, pecking him on the lips.

That afternoon, Zadie held her violin on her shoulder, stroking it with the bow, as she played “Spring La Primavera” in a recording studio. She smiled at Loco while she played the tune. Loco felt like the luckiest guy to have such a well-rounded girlfriend. A group of wannabe rappers from Harlem wanted to collaborate with her on music. She then played "Winter" by Vivaldi, and Loco raised his brows in amazement at how she could switch from one tune to another. He wasn't very familiar with classical music or the artsy crowd, but Zadie did.

A young Malevolent entered the studio, hearing the sweet notes of the violin echoing throughout the building. He maneuvered through the crowd of ruffians to his best friend's side, where Loco acknowledged him with a fist bump.

"What's going on, man?" Malevolent whispered.

"Same shit. Check out my girl," Loco nudged Malevolent.

Zadie then played "Summer" by Vivaldi on her violin as she poured her heart into the performance. Loco admired her confidence, noting how Zadie's smirk and attitude reflected that of a professional artist. While she performed, Loco and Malevolent whispered to each other.

"Do you want to use her on your tracks, Mal?" Loco kept one eye on Zadie but turned to look at Malevolent.

"I'm not ready yet." Malevolent shaking his head.

"What do you mean you're not ready?" Loco arched his eyebrow.

"I don't know, man," Malevolent shrugged.

"Why are you doubting yourself, yo? You've got some excellent material," Loco encouraged.

"Who wants to hear about my life?" Malevolent said.

"Believe me, a lot of people can relate. You wrote from your heart. What are you going to write about? Something stupid?" Loco shook his head at Malevolent's doubt.

During a recording session, a cornrowed rapper named “Poppie” from Bushwick, Brooklyn—a half-African-American, half-Puerto Rican artist—rapped his song "Praise" into a vintage microphone. Zadie stood on the other side, wearing headsets and holding her violin. She played a beautiful melody as the boom-bap beat was added to the track. The studio engineer adjusted the buttons on the soundboard, alongside Loco, Malevolent, and a large group of onlookers. Loco watched Poppie spit some fierce lyrics, unfazed by anything. He knew his best friend could do it; he just allowed Malevolent to take his time. Loco shifted his gaze to Zadie, unable to stop smiling at how expertly she handled the violin.

A few nights later at a Brooklyn nightclub, a thirteen-by-fourteen-inch photo banner of Poppie hung on the wall for his album release party. Hip-hop music blasted from the speakers as the DJ mixed tracks. A cameraman snapped photos of Loco, Poppie, and Malevolent, posing for the camera. This was Poppie's time to shine, not Loco's, but he still made it about him. Malevolent noticed what Loco was doing and laughed as he eased his way out of the shot. Zadie waltzed in with a drink in her hands, wearing a long black skirt and a silk pink blouse, her hair styled in a bun. She snapped her fingers, catching Loco's attention. He got the message, gave Poppie a fist bump, and stepped out of the frame. Zadie wrapped her arms around Loco as they kissed.

"Thank you, baby," Loco whispered in her ear as he took the drink from her hand.

"You're welcome," Zadie chuckled.

"And thanks to that violin of yours," he added.

"That old thing? It was nothing," Zadie shrugged.

"It was something. And you're something," Loco said, kissing her again.

Malevolent stood across the club with a drink in hand, watching his best friend and his girlfriend, all lovey-dovey. He sucked his teeth, placed his drink on a nearby table, and swaggered out of the club.

Loco blinked his eyes, sitting before his deceased girlfriend's picture in her family's living room. It felt as if she were there, watching him like an angel. Zadie's mannerisms, musical tastes, talents, and belief in God made her angelic. Mrs. Veico sashayed into the living room, a cup of hot tea in hand. "Lorenzo, here's some tea if you like," she said, placing the hot beverage on the glass table. Tears proceeded to drip down his face like a faucet.

Mrs. Veico wanted to congratulate Loco on his success in the music business, sensing he needed alone time with Zadie, even if only in spirit. She excused herself, aware that her daughter had company, leaning into the deeper connection they shared. Loco gazed into his girlfriend's photo, bowed his head, sobbing.

THE PAST

In a recording booth, Poppie rapped lyrics from another song titled "I'm the Illest." Again, Loco and Malevolent sat behind the large soundboard, nodding their heads to the music. Everything sounded great from this new artist, and Loco was grateful to work with such talent. He looked at Malevolent, who clearly enjoyed the performance, and nudged him.

"When are you going to get in that booth, Mal?" Loco rocked in his chair.

"I do not know," Malevolent shrugged.

"Would you stop procrastinating? Get in there!" Loco urged, rocking faster.

"When the time comes, when the time comes," Malevolent replied.

Then Loco's cell phone vibrated on his hip. He answered the call; the caller ID read: Mrs. Veico.

"Hello," Loco answered, his eyes widening as Mrs. Veico's voice trembled on the other end. He gasped, storming out of the studio.

"Shit! Mrs. Veico, calm down! I'll be there!" he rushed out of the building.

Paramedics rushed Zadie into the emergency room on a gurney, with Loco and Zadie's parents right behind them. Doctors and nurses surrounded her, providing medical assistance. Loco embraced Mrs. Veico as she sobbed uncontrollably. Mr. Veico paced the tiled floor, shaking his head. "My daughter! My daughter!" Loco couldn't believe what was happening. Was that somber solo Zadie had performed a foreshadowing? Or was it something else?

Loco's heart raced. Mrs. Veico told him Zadie had brain tumor; he was stunned and couldn't grasp it. Zadie had passed out in school during music class, violin in hand, pleading with her parents not to tell Lorenzo, fearing it would lose him. Loco shook his head in disbelief. *How could this happen to the woman he loved? The woman he hoped to spend the rest of his life with and have children.* Then a thin gentleman approached—Doctor Eisen—with a chart in hand. Loco and Zadie's parents looked to the doctor, hoping for better news, but the revelation was grim: Zadie had a cancerous tumor in the middle of her head. If they performed surgery, she could die on the table, and without the surgery, she would still die.

"Can we see her?" Loco asked.

The doctor nodded, but one person at a time. Loco suggested Mr. and Mrs. Veico see Zadie first. He leaned against the wall, sliding down to the floor as tears streamed down his face. Then his cell phone vibrated. Caller ID read: Malevolent.

"Yeah, Mal?"

"What happened, Loco?" Malevolent's voice echoed through the phone.

"Zadie's sick!"

"Zadie's sick? How?"

"She's got a tumor," Loco managed, his voice trembling as he balled his fist.

"When did this happen? Holy shit! I'm sorry, Loco," Malevolent's voice trailed off.

Loco sobbed, unable to respond.

"Hello? Loco! Loco! Answer me!" Malevolent's voice echoed through the receiver. In a fit of despair, Loco threw his cell against the wall, not caring if it hit anyone. He wished he could have caught Zadie in his arms before she fell.

PRESENT

"Lorenzo! Lorenzo!" a feminine voice called his name. Loco jarred awake, realizing he was still sitting on the sofa across from Zadie's urn. Her smiling photo scared him a bit, but he pushed the thought away. He feared she would haunt him for not being there when she needed him. Zadie was a beautiful and talented young woman with big dreams, paired with a boyfriend sharing similar goals. But death had knocked on her door and taken her away forever.

Loco missed her smile, laughter, corny jokes, and the way she stroked her bow on the violin. Now, Zadie was in heaven, playing for God. Since her death, Loco hadn't used Zadie's violin tracks in the music he produced for the rap artists he worked with. Loco stood from the chair. "Mrs. Veico, I'm sorry. I'm going now, and thank you for the tea!"

Hopefully, Mr. Veico would arrive home soon so Zadie's mother wouldn't be alone. Loco and Mr. Veico didn't see eye to eye; he believed the entire rap genre was bullshit, criticizing its themes of poverty, drugs, and disrespect towards women. Mr. Veico wanted Zadie to be with someone who shared her interests, and while Loco had things in common with her, he knew he wasn't what Mr. Veico envisioned.

Mrs. Veico rushed back into the living room as Loco pecked her on the cheek, sorrowful tears sliding down his face. He then blew a kiss at Zadie's picture before storming out of the house.

CHAPTER TEN

On an ominous music video set, a dark-haired boy tossed and turned in his twin-sized bed, hearing his father's cries echoing through the house. The boy's bedroom had blue walls, a toy chest in the corner filled with once-beloved items he no longer cared for, and a small desk holding a letter for his mother. As his father's voice grew louder, the boy actor sprang from his bed. A cameraman tracked the young actor's movements toward the bedroom door. "And cut!" the director shouted. Applause erupted from the camera crew, Malevolent, Portia, Loco, and the rest of the production team. Malevolent swaggered over to the young actor, named Julio, shaking his hand in congratulations. Earlier, he had spoken to Julio about his Hollywood dreams. The boy admired actors like Emilio Rivera, Denzel Washington, Tom Cruise, Vin Diesel, and many others. He had auditioned for commercials, television shows, and movies, traveling to California several times with his family for auditions in Tinseltown. It was a tough business. Malevolent's music video *"Boom! In the Night"* would be this young actor's big break, just as it would be a big break for

Malevolent himself, alongside "The Boom-Bap" and other tracks.

While Malevolent and Julio chatted, Portia stood in the background, giving him space. Malevolent knew he had to make more time for her, but his tight schedule left little room for movies, dinners, or intimacy. He needed to figure something out.

During the production crew's thirty-minute break, Malevolent and Portia cuddled at a small table while eating lunch. The couple exchanged no words, awestruck by the scope of the video production. Malevolent couldn't voice his feelings; the reenactment of his father's death weighed heavily on him. A severe sadness gripped his chest, the worst feeling in the world. Portia noticed the pain on his face, sensing he wanted to cry. All Malevolent could do was gaze at the set.

"Are you alright, baby?" Portia asked, rubbing his face. Malevolent looked her in the eyes.

"What do you think?" he responded softly. His gaze drifted to the camera crew preparing for the next scene. He felt an urge to kick the thirty-five-millimeter Arriflex camera and stomping it. But he didn't want to risk everything he had worked so hard for. The best he could do was take a walk, yet he remained in his chair as professionals recreated the most painful moment of his childhood. Malevolent knew all about the executives, producers, and sharks in the entertainment industry who profited from an artist's pain. He wondered, *"What was he going to do about it?" If he dared to confront these gentlemen about their greed, he'd regret it. Even Loco would be angry.*

Speaking of Loco, he mingled with three young ruffians, who pointed a camera and shoved a microphone in his face. Malevolent figured these guys were hip-hop radio station reporters, eager for the latest scoop. They wanted to know more about this new twenty-first-century hip-hop duo from

Queens who brought the Boom-Bap sound. The reporters approached Malevolent and Portia's table, the cameraman shoving the camera in his face, its bright light causing him to squint. The hip-hop reporter peppered him with questions about "Boom! In the Night!" and the music video.

Malevolent fought back tears as he took his time answering the questions but didn't allow these reporters to overstep their boundaries. He skillfully redirected them to his other songs, such as "Boom-Bap" and "Mourning Rose," and they followed his lead. Not far away, Portia and Loco stood in the background. He turned his attention to Portia, eyeing her from head to toe as he leaned in to whisper sweet nothings in her ear. Malevolent frowned during his interview, still hearing questions about his childhood.

"I really don't want to get into that right now," Malevolent said, annoyance creeping into his voice. He glared at the reporter, noticing Loco slipping his arm around Portia's waist. She gently pushed his hand away, rejecting his advances. As usual, Loco laughed it off and kept his hands to himself. Playing it cool, Loco gave Malevolent a thumbs-up as the interview wrapped up. Malevolent shot him a sneer and grabbed Portia's hand like a child reclaiming a toy.

"You did beautifully, man," Loco noted, observing Malevolent's abrupt dismissal of praise.

"Action!" the video director shouted later. Julio, the young child actor portraying Malevolent as a child, crept toward the bedroom. Malevolent, Loco, and Portia sat behind the camera with the film crew. Julio (Young Alejandro) opened the door, peering into the hallway. "BOOM!" The loud gunshot startled the child actor, freezing him in place. His heart raced in rhythm with Malevolent's, reliving the nightmare and stormed off the set. Portia attempted to follow him, but Loco grabbed her arm and pulled her towards him. "Give him time, Portia."

"Don't grab me like that!" she wrestled her arm from his grip, proceeding to run after Malevolent.

"I'm sorry, Portia," Loco sighed, sucking his teeth.

Malevolent's Dodge Challenger sped out of the parking lot of Silvercup Studios in Long·Island City. Portia was too late; the muscle car's wheels left a cloud of smoke in its wake. She stomped her foot, frustrated. *"What was the problem?"* she thought. She wanted to help Malevolent with his struggles, but maybe it was best to let him be. Turning around, she saw Loco exiting the studio building. She stood frozen in place, unable to move. Loco swaggered toward her with a fiendish grin, sending her heart racing and her eyes brimming with tears. He cradled her in his arms, not saying a word, but his actions spoke volumes. Portia felt his strong, muscular chest against her body. Again, she wrestled out of his strong embrace.

"I'm with Malevolent. I can't," Portia protested, storming past him and back into the building.

Raindrops streamed down Portia's bedroom window that night as she tossed and turned in bed, replaying the day's events. She didn't want to intrude on Malevolent and Loco's dreams, and their dream wasn't hers. Portia needed to focus more on her own aspirations, but Loco wanted her to help finish the album. She knew she had to extricate herself from this situation before it worsened. Portia was always worried about what lay ahead. The only thing she needed to do was focus on her craft. Her piano playing helped her unwind and think about the larger world. Thank God for his creation—the world to see, live, and dream in.

Portia sat upright in bed, throwing the blanket off. She glanced at her cell phone on her nightstand but hesitated to reach for it. Curiosity bloomed inside her as she wondered if Malevolent had called. Her heart raced, as though she were stepping into a nightmare. Taking a deep breath, she finally snatched the phone. After pressing the button to turn it on, she found no calls or voicemails from Malevolent. Her determination surged as she dialed his number. The phone rang repeatedly, but there was no response. She ended the call and tried again, but it rang and rang, still no answer. Then it went to voicemail.

"Yo! This is Malevolent. Leave your name and number, and I'll holla back at you! Peace!" BEEP!

Portia took a moment to gather her thoughts. The light static of the voicemail recording crackled in her ear as she prepared to speak.

"Malevolent! This is Portia. Why did you leave the set? The director was looking for you to see the playback of the video. Everything came out pretty good, especially Julio's performance. He'll be the next A-list actor in Hollywood," Portia's voice quivered. "Baby, please call me back!"

She ended the call and placed the phone back on her nightstand. Resting her arm behind her head, Portia gazed at the ceiling and shut her eyes.

Meanwhile Malevolent tapped the keys of the computer at the desk in the supermarket manager's office. The room was dimly lit, illuminated only by a lamp in the corner. His cellphone vibrated, alerting him of a new voicemail. He glanced at the small screen but then returned to his work.

“Good night, Alejandro!” said a female store manager

carrying her purse and shopping bags as she peeked into the office and waved.

"Get home safe, Natasha," Malevolent replied, waving and smiling. He looked at the clock on the wall; it was almost closing time.

"Attention all shoppers! Just Rite will be closing in thirty minutes! Please bring your items to the last register to be checked. And thanks for shopping at Just Rite, the friendliest store in Queens!" Malevolent announced over the loudspeaker. He switched it off and walked out of the office into the well-lit store, where a few shoppers had carts full of food. He didn't understand how some people shopped at eleven-thirty at night; he knew it was none of his business. His task was to ensure the night crew was prepped to stock items, clean the store, and complete other duties for the next business morning. He swaggered into the deli, greeting his co-workers, who were cleaning the meat slicer and glass counter and storing deli meats in the cooler. "What's up, Juan?" Malevolent waved at a tall, skinny young man in his mid-twenties.

"How did your music video go? I heard it was cool!"

"It went smoothly, and my recording sessions as well!" Malevolent nodded.

"I'm looking forward to the release of your first single!" the young deli worker exclaimed.

"I'll keep you posted! Talk to you later!" Malevolent said.

"Check you out later, Mal!" Juan went back to his tasks.

A sweet aroma filled the air as Malevolent passed by the bakery. Dolores, a pretty young woman with a slight Caribbean accent, rushed to him with open arms and kissed him on the cheek. "Alejandro! How are you? How is your music going?" she asked, pulling off her plastic gloves.

"I just wrapped up my music video and got more tracks to

record. Hopefully, I'll complete the album," Malevolent shrugged, not feeling very certain.

"I believe in you. You're going to be a big star," Dolores kissed him again.

"Thank you, babe," Malevolent smiled.

"There are some more donuts and pastries if you'd like," she pointed to the bakery department.

"Cool," he replied, beginning to swagger away.

"I'll leave some in the back for you. I'll be closing soon," Dolores hurried back into the bakery. Malevolent strolled into the produce department, noticing the new employees stocking more fruits and vegetables for the last customers shopping. He greeted the employees with smiles as he made his rounds toward the front end of the store. He nodded at the girl at self-checkout, who was assisting a customer with their groceries. "How are you?" Malevolent greeted, noticing another new face. He observed the long line of cash registers, where actual humans served shoppers. As the store prepared to close for the night, only three registers had cashiers along with two front-end managers ensuring everything ran smoothly. As Malevolent swaggered through the automatic double doors, he forgot it had rained. Stepping onto the damp concrete, he waved to the cart attendant, who was wheeling four carts pushed together across the lot.

He glanced at his watch; it was only twenty minutes before closing. Grabbing his keys from his pocket, he aimed them at his vehicle, unlocking it. He swung the driver's side door open, hopped in and closed it. Malevolent dialed Portia's number on his cell and waited for an answer. On the first ring, he found success.

"Malevolent!" a feminine, exhausted voice answered.

"Yes, it's me!" Malevolent exhaled.

"Why did you storm off like that?" Portia cried.

“Why would you allow Loco to touch you like that?” Malevolent asked in a stern tone.

“I pushed him away!” Portia shouted while her voice quivered.

“Don’t yell in my ear!” Malevolent punched the steering wheel.

“I’m not yelling at you! Are we serious about each other, or do you just want to get in my pants?” Portia whined.

“No! You mean something to me!” Malevolent spoke in a soothing tone. “Maybe I should’ve been a little more vocal. I’m sorry,” he sighed.

“Well, actions speak louder than words,” Portia added.

“You’re right, baby. I’ll talk to you later,” Malevolent leaned back in the driver’s seat, lightly punching the steering wheel.

“Okay, have a good shift, and stay safe,” Portia replied in whined voice.

“Good night, baby. I’ll see you at the studio,” Malevolent spoke in a loving tone.

“Good night,” Portia said before hanging up.

Malevolent ended the call and leaned back in the driver’s seat, contemplating *"Actions speaking louder than words."* He exited his car and rushed into the supermarket, ready for his shift.

CHAPTER ELEVEN

In a recording studio days later, Malevolent stood before a vintage microphone wearing headphones, joined by hip-hop legend Joe Jose. Clothed in dark attire, the artists stood against the soundproofed walls, creating an intense atmosphere. The collaboration's early arrival surprised Malevolent, but Loco's quick networking made it happen.

Miss me wit the bullshit,
I ain't new to this,
I was born for this,
Lights! Camera! Money! Fame!
Action!
And all that good shit.
Malevolent is my name, and hip-hop fame is a game.
Chess!
Not checkers!"

With an aggressive style, Malevolent performed his self-written rap. As he rapped, he noticed Joe was impressed with his skills. Through the glass window, Loco gave him a thumbs up. A smug expression surfaced on Malevolent's face as he continued. The thirty-five mm Arriflex Steadicam wobbled in front of him in the cramped recording booth. Malevolent concluded his verse, and the camera turned to Joe Jose, spitting his explicit lyrics into the vintage microphone with a pop filter.

Fuck that shit!
I've never been mother fuckin' new to this shit!
I'm coming from the Bronx
Birth of Hip Hop,
It never stopped,
Especially me, Joe Jose,
What more can I say,
Born in Bronx dale,
Growing up in the rough streets
seeing hoodboogas,
good guys, bad guys,
cops and robbers,
a typical Bronx tale, not like the movie,
but my version,
this place being my home,"

Joe Jose continued with his verse, while fans, friends, hangers-on, and studio personnel sat behind the soundboard, nodding to the music. Even amid Malevolent's performance, he hoped Portia would come to work, or maybe she would call out sick. On top of this duet with Joe Jose, Loco had also booked him to perform in the Puerto Rican Day parade. He would talk to Malevolent about it after the recording session and music video.

"Shout out to Queens!"
"Shout out to the boogie down Bronx!"

Over the boom-bap beat, Malevolent and Joe Jose's echoing voices sounded quite sinister. Loco, Benji, studio engineers, and his entourage applauded another job well done. From his recliner, Loco swaggered to the booth as Malevolent stepped out, and the cameraman backed away. The cameraman panned the Steadicam on Loco and Malevolent, who bumped fists. Loco then bumped fists with Joe Jose as he exited the booth. The collaboration's success received praise, fist bumps, and hugs from everyone.

Slipping into the recording studio, Portia saw a huge throng of Malevolent's new fans. She could tell they were a new set of onlookers—too many for her comfort. Two star-struck guys from Malevolent's neighborhood strolled past her, carrying a video camera. Unsure of their professional intentions, she knew her lover would soon be famous. Once again, Malevolent was busy with admirers, mostly beautiful women—more attractive than Jazzy at his last music video shoot. From the background, Portia watched as if she were witnessing a moment in Malevolent's life, standing alone. His hip-hop journey was just beginning, filled with promise and excitement. From afar, she stared into his eyes, hoping he felt her gaze. But no. Malevolent basked in the attention, oblivious to her presence. Tears welled in Portia's eyes while her heart raced, and stormed out of the studio.

Seconds later, Portia hung her purse and jacket on the coat rack at the front desk as she greeted her colleague, Tony.

Trying to hold back tears, she managed a tight smile. Although Tony wanted to know what was wrong, he didn't ask.

"Aren't you curious about what's troubling me?" Portia punched the desk and sobbed. Tony offered a calming touch on her shoulder. Crying her eyes out, Portia put her head down on the desk. Loco approached the front desk, noticing Portia in tears. "Portia, sweetheart, what is it?" He kneeled beside her, rubbing her back and inching his hand down her lower back. Loco planted a kiss on her cheek.

"Get away from me! I'm going to find another job!" Portia stood up, grabbing her jacket and purse, rushing out of the building.

"No! Don't!" Loco pursued her.

In a matter of minutes, Portia hurried toward the subway on Queens Boulevard as Loco ran behind her and blocked her path. He again pulled her close and kissing her.

"What the hell! Leave me alone, Loco!" Portia exclaimed, wiggled her from his arms.

"You and Malevolent aren't even official! Relationships in this business are temporary. What you have with him is a situationship, Portia!" Loco raised his voice while the rumble of the elevated subway train drowned out his words. Portia continued into the train station, not glancing back at him.

Loco glared at Portia as she ascended the steel steps into the train station. He inhaled sharply, then spit a glob of mucus on the concrete before rushing back to the studio. "Fuck!"

That night, Portia paced her wooden-floored bedroom, engaged in a phone argument with Loco. Ignoring each other's feelings, the two exchanged meaningless words. Portia attempted to make Loco understand her disinterest.

"You sure do live in La-La Land! Portia, I can do more for you than he can! I can give you the world!" Loco insisted, fueling his pursuit.

"I don't want your world!" she cut him off.

"I can make things very bad for you," Loco's voice sounded threatening.

"Why are you doing this to me? Are you threatening my livelihood?" Portia's voice quivered as she sobbed. "You're a snake! And you're crazy!" she hollered into her cellphone.

"And that's why they call me DJ Loco—because I'm dope on the turntables, and I fight for what I want!" Portia only heard gibberish from Loco. Her focus was on not waking her parents. She tiptoed to her bedroom door and cracked it open.

"Portia!" Loco called her name. She didn't respond. Her eyes locked onto the master bedroom door down the murky hallway of the second floor, illuminated only by a glowing nightlight and the TV playing in her parents' room. Gently, she closed her bedroom door.

"Portia! Answer me!" Loco demanded.

"Who do you think you are? You don't own me!" Portia sat on the edge of her bed. She wept as tears trickled down her face like a faucet.

"The reason I'm pursuing you is because..."

"I don't care! I'm not settling for you! I don't care how much money you have or your success," Portia ended the call and slammed it on the nightstand. Even though Loco was a successful music producer and a philanderer, he was unsuitable for an introduction to her parents. Just then, her cell vibrated on the nightstand, almost falling off. She caught it in the palm of her hand. The caller ID read: Malevolent. She quickly answered.

"Hello, Malevolent!"

"Yes, baby. It's me. I'm outside!" he said.

"Okay!" she quickly hung up, putting on her light robe. Portia then crept downstairs and exited the front door.

Outside the Fairchild residence, the monstrous Challenger vehicle was parked directly in front of her house. Surprisingly, Portia hadn't heard its rumbling engine. As Malevolent lounged in the driver's seat, he dimmed the headlights and unlocked the passenger door for Portia as she hopped in. Immediately, they lip-locked, forgetting about the neighbors watching as their passion ignited. Heavy breathing and moans emerged between them as Malevolent inched his hand up Portia's pajama top. She wore no bra, and he pinched her nipples, his hand traveling down her thigh and toward her vaginal area. The time read ten-twenty p.m. Malevolent noticed the time on his dashboard; he had plenty of time to get to work and could use a bit of intimacy right now. However, Portia didn't want the neighbors to catch her and her boyfriend getting hot and heavy in his vehicle; she would be mortified if it went viral on social media.

Just as Malevolent's finger was about to enter her, Portia pushed his hand away. "Baby, not here!" she protested, pulling away from him.

"I'm sorry. Are you quitting on me, Portia?" he asked, planting a peck on her lips.

"No, I'm not quitting on you," she laughed it off.

"I heard you're looking for another job," Malevolent raised an eyebrow.

"Yeah, sometime in the near future," she responded shyly.

"You're quitting on my project? I need you, Portia," Malevolent laid a passionate kiss on her again. "Showing her, how much he needed her." both musically and romantically. They gazed into each other's eyes, sharing a loving embrace.

"Tell me something. What was Loco whispering in your ear?" Malevolent whispered.

Portia released herself from his embrace and focused her eyes in the opposite direction. He could tell by her demeanor that Loco had said something that got under her skin. Malevolent remembered how hard he worked to get this album completed. With Portia adding her special touch, he had to keep his cool.

"Baby, you don't have to answer that. I'll take care of it," Malevolent said, touching her chin and leaning in for another kiss.

"Please don't do anything stupid. I don't want to mess things up for you. You've got your album coming out, and you've already filmed two music videos and are about to drop a couple of singles. Don't risk it," Portia grasped his hand.

"I promise, I won't. If I see it again, it's going to be hell. Shit, we've been down this road before," Malevolent shook his head, looking away.

"I don't mean to cause any trouble. I don't want to break up your friendship," Portia said, paranoid. He reassured her that this situation had nothing to do with her.

"Another triangle," he mumbled.

"What?" Portia lifted an eyebrow.

"This could be my third time experiencing this," Malevolent glared at her directly in the eyes, as if he was ready to divulge details.

"A love triangle? How?" Portia shrugged.

"It's a long story starting with my parents..." Malevolent inhaled as tears welled in his eyes. Portia immediately wiped them away while they streamed down his face.

"I'm so sorry," Portia got choked up as well. Malevolent noticed her tears cascading down her cheeks and, in return, wiped her tears away.

"Don't cry, baby," he repeatedly kissed her on the cheek. He realized it was time to get going to work. He gave her one last kiss on the forehead and started the engine.

"I'll tell you the rest of the story later," he whispered.

"Good night," Portia exited the car, dashing into the house, waving at him before closing the door. The monstrous car sped off into the night.

CHAPTER TWELVE

In the early morning hours at the supermarket, Malevolent scanned the canned goods with the scan gun. He stocked cans of vegetables on the shelf alongside his colleagues. He glanced at his watch; it read 5:35 a.m. It was almost time to open the supermarket for business. He got off at six-thirty and needed sleep, but he had to get to the recording studio. Malevolent couldn't wait until he could resign from this job so he could fully focus on his music career. Things were looking up, but trouble was brewing. After work, Malevolent planned to visit Portia's house. He didn't want to come off as paranoid or smothering, but he didn't want to lose her to Loco. Loco had plenty of women—like Jazzy, who was nothing compared to Zadie. Portia was the closest thing to Zadie for Malevolent. He wanted Portia to meet his family and get to know him better, the positive things. He didn't have to work the next night, so he and Portia would have plenty of time to spend together.

"Good morning, Mr. Alejandro!" Natasha marched toward him with a price gun in hand, ready for the day.

"What's going on?" Malevolent yawned.

"It's been a long night! I know!" Natasha smiled as if she didn't have a care in the world.

"I'm almost out of here," he yawned again and rubbed his eyes like a baby.

"How's the music going?" she asked.

"It's going well. Pretty soon I'll be on tour with some of the big wigs in the industry," Malevolent smiled.

"Or they will be on stage with you. Remember, always play it cool as if you've already made it," Natasha encouraged.

"Yes, good advice," Malevolent nodded.

Later that morning, the Dodge Challenger parked in front of the Fairchild residence as Malevolent exited the driver's seat. Portia's neighborhood was quiet, only the birds sang with a Yorkie barking from across the street. The tiny, sharp, yaps caused him to glance over his shoulder because little dogs can be more aggressive than the bigger ones. Malevolent didn't call Portia to let her know he was coming; it was very early, and he hoped she wouldn't mind. He trotted to the front door and rang the bell. Rubbery slippers shuffled along the wooden floor, as an enormous figure swung open the front door. Once again, Malevolent and Mr. Fairchild eyed each other for a moment without saying a word. The man of the house, dressed in night clothes, widened the door and beckoned Malevolent to enter. Malevolent swaggered in and nodded to him in thanks.

As he waltzed into the living room, a strong aroma of coffee filled the air. Mr. Fairchild offered him a seat. "Would you like some coffee, Alejandro?"

"Yes, thanks," Malevolent replied with a slight smile, plopping down on the couch.

"Portia! Alejandro's here!" Mr. Fairchild shouted from the bottom of the staircase and then marched into the kitchen.

"Okay!" Portia shouted from the second floor. She hurried downstairs with open arms for Malevolent. They engaged in a passionate kiss, almost forgetting her parents were present.

"Good morning, babe!" Portia chuckled.

"Same to you, Portia," he said, laying a kiss on her forehead. Mr. Fairchild returned with a steaming coffee mug in his hand. The couple released each other from their embrace.

"Don't mind me. I know you two are in love," Mr. Fairchild said, offering the coffee mug to Malevolent.

"Thank you," he nodded.

"You're welcome. Enjoy the rest of your day," Portia's father stomped upstairs.

Malevolent took a sip of the hot cup of joe and smiled.

"You like it?" Portia asked.

"Yes! It's that vanilla creamer I love," he replied.

"I prefer hazelnut," Portia smiled.

"Portia, get dressed," Malevolent said, handing her the coffee mug.

"Where are we going?" Portia asked, wrapping her arm around his waist and kissing him.

"Somewhere. I'll figure it out," Malevolent shrugged.

Later that morning, Malevolent and Portia held hands while carrying shopping bags from Bath and Body Works and Macy's. They strolled through a not-so-crowded shopping mall; it wasn't the weekend, but it was close. Malevolent gulped down an iced coffee from a plastic cup, crunching the ice between his teeth.

"Holy shit!" he tossed the cold brew into the trash can.

"What's wrong?" Portia followed him to the trash can.

"The ice is too cold against my teeth," Malevolent said, clutching Portia's hand.

"Where are we off to now?" Portia giggled.

"In here," Malevolent led her into the fabulous Zales jewelry store. Inside, the establishment displayed cases of diamonds, pearls, and other jewels that was—every girl's best friend. Malevolent didn't know exactly what he was going to get Portia, but it was going to be something special. He could sense that Portia seemed nervous, likely thinking he would ask for her hand in marriage. But it was too soon for that.

A glasses-clad, slender woman stood behind the counter of sparkling diamonds. "How are you, sir? Are you looking for something special?" the jeweler greeted.

"Yes, I am," Malevolent said, pulling Portia close to him.

"We have beautiful jewels for that special someone," the jeweler browsed through the glass case. "What exactly are you looking for?"

"A ring," Malevolent answered.

Portia remained silent, frowning as Malevolent noticed her odd behavior and hoped it wouldn't freak her out. His eyes widened at the sparkling selection of rings that could be for engagement, wedding, or just something special. It didn't matter; all he knew was that Portia was worth every penny. He pointed at a large diamond silver ring, glancing at the price. Yes, it was expensive, but Portia deserved it.

"Ma'am, can I see that ring?" Malevolent asked the jeweler.

She unlocked the glass case and presented the ring to him. Just looking at the glistening jewel made him want Portia to be in his life forever. He saw Portia browsing jewels on the other side. "Portia, come here," he called.

She waltzed over and leaned close to him. "Yes, Mal?" she replied sweetly.

Malevolent took her hand and slipped the expensive ring onto her finger.

"What's this?" she asked, surprised.

"We're official. We're a couple," he said, kissing her on the lips. He then tossed his credit card on the counter. "Charge it to my card."

That night, the Dodge Challenger parked before the Valasquez Residence, a small house on a street in Rego Park, Queens. A rottweiler barked from across the street, loud music played, and neighbors made clamored in the distance. Every room in the Valasquez home was lit as Malevolent and Portia exited the car. Malevolent grabbed her by the waist and marched to the front door. He rang the doorbell and despite the loud music in the distance, Pop music was almost as loud from inside of the home.

"Abuelo! It's me!" he called, knocking on the screen door. Portia glanced over her shoulder., noticing his neck of the woods was a bit louder. The front door swung open with squeaking hinges.

"What?!" Erasmo shouted.

Portia screamed, grabbing Malevolent's shirt.

"It's me," Malevolent said quickly.

"Alejandro! What the hell is your problem breaking down my door!" Erasmo widened the screen door, inviting Malevolent and Portia to enter.

"Hello! How are you?" his grandfather greeted Portia.

Once inside, Malevolent and Portia stepped into the living room, holding hands. Malevolent spotted his grandmother, Martha, dancing in the kitchen. She waved at him, and the atmosphere in his grandparents' home was filled with music, laughter, love, and happiness. Martha danced towards her grandson, embracing him with a hug and a kiss. "How's my favorite grandbaby?"

"I can't complain," Malevolent sighed.

"That's great to hear! He's going to be the next international hip-hop star like Drake, Big Pun, and all the other artists!" Martha kept dancing, noticing Portia standing in the background with a smile. "Hello!"

"How are you?" Portia greeted shyly.

"This is Portia, Abuela!" Malevolent introduced.

"How are you? She's the one that plays piano?" his grandmother asked.

"Yes, she's excellent. Portia can play anything," Malevolent said, puffing out his chest and giving Portia a kiss on the cheek.

"I always wanted to play the piano. I never got a chance," Erasmo said, scratching his head while leaning against the wall, regretting not pursuing the craft.

"It's never too late," Portia encouraged.

"Let's discuss music over dinner. I've got a roast in the oven!" Martha danced her way back into the kitchen.

"Have a seat," Malevolent's grandfather pointed toward the sofa. Portia and Malevolent planted themselves on the comfy furniture.

"Would you like something to drink, Portia?" Erasmo asked.

"Yes, a water is fine," Portia smiled.

"You got it," Erasmo snapped his fingers as he dragged his rubbery slippers along the floor, making a screeching sound.

While Malevolent and Portia sat on the couch, no words exchanged just smiles and glances. The Valasquez's living room was the typical set up with the sofa that they lounged on, a glass coffee table adorned with several figurines, a ballerina,

Jesus, Puerto Rican Coqui frog on a tree branch, and clear glass glittery red roses. Portia's eyes scanned the warm setting, noticing the Puerto Rican flag on the wall, a small grandfather clock, and dozens of family photos from the walls and throughout the house. There were pictures of Malevolent's father, grandparents, aunts, uncles, cousins and his friends. On top of that, there were more photos of Malevolent's baby pictures to the present day, his karate and Kung Fu tournaments, and three trophies that he won. Portia's jaw dropped, seeing his high school graduation picture in an eight-by-ten frame.

"Is that you, Mal?" Portia pointed.

"Yes, that's me," Malevolent yawned.

Portia rushed over and held the large photo, gazing at it in admiration. He looked just as handsome in high school as he did now. *"How many girls had a crush on him back then?"* she wondered. Portia caressed her fingers over the photo, smiling. She reaffirmed to herself that she had nothing to worry about; Malevolent was her man. She placed the framed picture on the table and noticed his baby pictures.

"You were such a beautiful baby," Portia sighed as she noticed his childhood pictures with a man. "Is that your father?"

"Yes," he exhaled.

"You look exactly like him," she added while proceeded to browse, noticing there were no pictures of his mother. She wanted to ask, but it was none of her business. Portia then came across Malevolent and Loco's pictures from high school, chilling in the park, at home working on music at home or in the recording studio, and even a picture of the best friends at the club.

"You and Loco have a long history," Portia said.

"Yes, we do," Malevolent shrugged.

“Did you take Martial Arts?” Portia dashed to Malevolent’s Karate pictures and read the awards with his name on them.

“Yes. I wanted to be like Jackie Chan,” Malevolent chuckled.

“Rush Hour must be your favorite movie,” Portia smiled.

“Yeah, it’s on my playlist,” Malevolent said.

“Do you know how to use nunchucks and blades?” Portia asked.

“Yes,” he nodded.

“That’s why you made the song “Machete” Right?” she asked.

“Sort of,” Malevolent shrugged. He then pressed his strong body close while wrapping his strong arms around her waist. “Spend the night with me,” he whispered in her ear.

“Yes,” Portia whispered in return as they shared a kiss.

Just then, Erasmo’s rubbery slippers squeaked against the wooden floor again as he entered the living room with a bottled water in hand.

“Oh, I see you like our family pics. We have so many more family albums that you can see, his grandfather laughed proudly. “Here you go,” Erasmo offered the bottled water to Portia.

“Thank you so much,” she replied.

“Dinner is ready!” Martha hollered from the distance.

“Vamos!” Erasmo beckoned, making his way towards the dining room.

“I started playing piano at three years old,” Portia shared her musical journey while seated at Malevolent’s grandparents’ dining room table later. Erasmo, who sat at the head of the table, leaned forward and grasped Portia’s words intently. Malevolent noticed his grandfather’s behavior and hoped he wouldn't judge Portia for being an elitist. Portia spoke about her father being an Air Force veteran, her mother a homemaker, living in different countries, and her education at Oxford University, where she studied music. His grandparents exchanged glances, making faces as Malevolent sensed they probably doubted her lifestyle and might not like Portia.

"I would love to meet your father, Portia," Erasmo said.

"Of course, you can meet him anytime," Portia replied proudly.

"I met Mr. Fairchild several times," Malevolent said, sticking out his chest proudly.

"You have?" Erasmo asked doubtfully.

"Yes, I have," Malevolent leaned forward in his chair, taking a sip of his drink.

"Very interesting," Erasmo said, eyeing his wife.

"Sounds impressive," Martha added.

Running water poured from the kitchen faucet into a sink of dirty dishes as Martha washed them with a soapy sponge an hour later. Erasmo peeked into the living room from kitchen, eavesdropping on Malevolent and Portia flipping through the family albums. Erasmo crept to his wife's side. "Do you really believe her?"

"If Portia says her father was in the Air Force, I believe her," Martha said, lowering her voice as she placed a wet dish in the rack. "What's the problem?"

"I don't have a problem," Erasmo shrugged. He peeked into the living room again while Portia and their grandson continued to look at the family albums.

"Why are you snooping, Erasmo?" Martha pulled him back into the kitchen with her wet hands.

"Your hands are wet!" Erasmo wiping the drips of water off himself.

"Of course, I'm washing dishes. I could get this done faster if you would stop being so nosy," Martha continued with the dishes.

"Did you see that ring on her finger?" Erasmo asked.

"What ring?" Martha's eyebrow arched.

"It looks like an engagement ring on her finger," Erasmo said as he dried the dishes, stacking them in the cabinet.

"Really?" Martha shoved a wet dish into the sink.

"Abuela, why didn't you ask me to help you with the dishes?" Alejandro swaggered into the kitchen.

"Don't worry, sweetheart. Your grandfather and I got this under control," Martha assured him.

Erasmo frowned as Alejandro chatting with his grandmother. Erasmo started to worry about this girl they just met—if she might be another woman playing with his grandson's heart.

"You're going to be a big star. I can't wait to see your name in lights," Martha said, laying a kiss on her grandson's cheek.

"I hope those lights are dimmed, Alejandro," Erasmo said, turning back to the shelf.

Alejandro raised an eyebrow at his grandfather's remark. "Que quieres decir?" (What do you mean?)

"Is that an engagement ring on her finger?" his grandfather asked.

"Yes, sort of," Alejandro replied casually.

"Sort of? Are you messing around with someone else's woman?" Erasmo pressed.

"Portia's mine! I bought her that ring," he glared at his grandfather.

"That's wonderful. How long have you been seeing her?" Martha asked.

"Not too long," Alejandro stuffing a cookie into his mouth from the glass cookie jar.

"Portia seems like a wonderful girl," Martha smiled.

"Be careful, Alejandro. Please," Erasmo's voice quivered, tears welling in his eyes. Erasmo's words reminded Alejandro of the tragedy he experienced as a child. "I wrote about that event in my music, and I'll never forget it," he said. Alejandro consoled his grandfather, patting him on the shoulder.

"It's going to be alright. Portia's a sweetheart," Alejandro assured him.

"I hope she cares about you, Alejandro. I hope she's not with you for your rise to fame," Erasmo focused on his duties. Martha abruptly shut the water off and embraced her husband. "Hopefully, everything will be fine. Alejandro made a good choice."

"Yes, I have," he shook his head. Alejandro glanced at his watch. "I've got to be going now."

As Alejandro swaggered into the living room, his grandparents followed behind. Portia placed the family album on the coffee table and stood up, noticing Alejandro approaching with open arms. He leaned in to kiss her.

"We've got to go."

"It was nice meeting you, Portia," Martha waved.

"Thank you for dinner, Mrs. Valasquez," Portia said, putting on her light jacket.

"Anytime. You and Alejandro can come over anytime. Don't be a stranger," Martha said.

Erasmo stood in the background, not saying a word as they mingled a bit. He didn't know what to think about that ring. Maybe it was fake, but that rock on her finger looked expensive. If Alejandro bought that ring for her, it probably emptied out his entire bank account.

"It was nice meeting you, Mr. Valasquez," Portia waved. She noticed Alejandro's grandfather's eyes were teary. Portia hoped she hadn't triggered him. Alejandro gave his grandfather one last hug before stepping out the door.

"If you need anything or run into any problems, contact me. You hear me?" Erasmo glared at his grandson directly in the eye.

"Yes, sir," Alejandro replied as he and his grandfather bumped fists. He then kissed his grandmother on the cheek.

"I love you, sweetheart. And let me hear some of your music," Martha said.

"Soon! Soon!" Alejandro trotted down the concrete steps, making his way to his car. Portia hopped into the passenger seat while he slid into the driver's seat. He revved the engine of his muscle car and sped off, honking the horn at his grandparents as a final goodbye.

An hour later, keys rattled at an apartment door that opened to a murky living room with dim lighting in the corner. Malevolent and Portia had their arms around each other, kissing, moaning, and groaning as they entered the darkened apartment.

"Babe, turn the lights on," Portia said.

Malevolent rubbed his hand along the wall, searching for the light switch, and the room illuminated. He then closed the door with his foot.

"Come here," Malevolent breathed heavily as he pulled Portia into his arms, kissing her as he reached his hand up her shirt, caressing her breasts. While the moaning and groaning continued, Malevolent removed her shirt and then unfastened her bra. He paused to admire her breasts. "You are so fuckin' beautiful," Malevolent murmured, sucking on her breast before unzipping her pants and pulling them down. He stripped off his shirt, pants, and boxers, becoming fully naked. Malevolent rushed Portia into the bedroom and pushed her onto his king-sized bed. She lay on her back as he inserted a finger into her, thrusting gently. Portia closed her eyes and took deep breaths. She noticed Malevolent's erect penis as he inserted it into her. He took deep, hard thrusts while she enjoyed every moment. They rolled over, with Portia now on top, thrusting away.

A couple of hours later, Malevolent stared at the ceiling, wide awake, while Portia slept like a baby. He couldn't understand why he was still awake after everything that had happened. He thought he'd be fast asleep, but instead, he stared at the ceiling with nothing on his mind. He figured the intimacy had cleared his head, but he suddenly remembered he owed Loco for leaving the studio and causing him money.

Sitting on the edge of his bed with the covers over his important parts, he reached for his boxers and slipped them on. He grabbed his cellphone, scrolled through his apps, and opened the Cash App. He sent eight hundred dollars to Loco.

"Now you've got your money," he whispered.

Portia stirred in the bed with the sheets over her body. She opened her eyes and saw Malevolent standing right at the foot of the bed.

"Mal," Portia sat upright, wiping her eyes.

"Yes, I'm here," he answered.

"Okay," Portia scratched her head. He couldn't help but notice how that jewel on her finger glistened.

"That ring looks good on you," Malevolent complimented with a smirk.

"This beauty? Thanks," Portia flashed the sparkling rock.

Malevolent swaggered to the bed side, standing there as he slid off his boxers and ready for round two. Portia couldn't help but notice his well-endowed man parts. Her cheeks blushed while she positioned herself in bed ready to go.

CHAPTER THIRTEEN

Loud rap music emanated from the speakers in the recording studio the next day, as the ceiling lights illuminated the grand piano in the instrument room. In the meeting room, a graphic artist was showcasing the album cover for Malevolent's next release, featuring a striking black rose paired with a vintage silver microphone. Loco glared at the black flower, its raindrops symbols of grief for his best friend's father. He could relate; he too suffered a loss and hoped for a better future. The dazzling retro microphone sparkled like a diamond on a woman's hand. He could have placed a wedding ring on Zadie's finger. Yes, that was the woman he lost to cancer, and he truly wished she had lived. He fist-bumped the designer for a job well done. The initial stages of the project thrilled him, and he eagerly awaited Malevolent's arrival. He glanced at the clock mounted on the wall; it read 8:15. Fingers crossed, Malevolent would arrive any moment now.

Just as he hoped, Malevolent and Portia entered the studio, their hands intertwined. Loco greeted Malevolent with an embrace and a fist bump.

While the two friends talked business, Portia concealed herself behind Malevolent. Avoiding Loco's gaze, she shifted her focus elsewhere. Despite her efforts, she couldn't evade the man who wouldn't take no for an answer.

Loco grinned wickedly. "Good morning, Portia."

She responded with a "Good morning," but kept a physical distance, her gaze fixed on anything but him.

Raising an eyebrow, Malevolent noticed the strange greeting they shared. "Did you receive the money I sent, Loco?" he inquired.

"Thanks, man," Loco replied, showing off the stunning album art. "Look at this, Mal."

"Wow! This is amazing!" Malevolent high-fived Loco.

Malevolent waved Portia over. "Honey, take a look!" Portia approached her boyfriend unhurriedly. Her eyes widened as she saw the dark, water-droplet rose beside the silver antique microphone.

"It's beautiful, Alejandro! This silver microphone is as shiny as my ring," Portia said, showing off her sparkling ring. Loco, the graphic designer, and Malevolent all observed the rock on her finger. Loco's heart thudded in his chest; his thoughts were in disarray. It was impossible for that to be an engagement ring—they had only just started dating and were still serious.

The hip-hop duo was then photographed by a cameraman who seemed to appear out of nowhere. Loco smiled, placing a hand on his best friend's shoulder. Malevolent was taken by surprise at the camera's blinding flash, catching him in a vulnerable moment, and he reacted with a sneer. He hadn't even noticed where the cameraman had been hiding. Obviously, he had been lurking around, waiting for Malevolent and Portia to waltz into the meeting room.

Malevolent then set his sights on his album and what it

was meant to convey: gloom, isolation, hopelessness, and even death. He felt compelled to be honest with his audience, believing they faced similar circumstances. Indirectly, his intention in flashing Portia's ring was to signal that he wanted her to marry him if his album became a huge hit. For a moment, Malevolent stared at the shining silver microphone.

"Yo, the cover is dope! It's gorgeous!" Malevolent exclaimed.

"You have every reason to be proud of yourself! You managed it!" Loco embraced his best friend.

"We've achieved it! We're a duo!" Malevolent guffawed. They exchanged fist bumps.

Next, the photographer continued to capture images of Malevolent and Loco side-by-side, while Portia remained in the background, observing her boyfriend and his best friend posing for the shots. She waved to them, giving a thumbs-up.

While the cameraman snapped pictures of the rap duo, Loco couldn't help but notice Portia's sparkling ring from a distance.

"How much do you think that ring is worth?" he wondered. He and Malevolent struck another cool pose, embodying hot masculinity. The photographer snapped multiple shots.

"Guys, give me another cool pose!" the cameraman insisted. Malevolent leaned his arm on Loco's shoulder, and Loco held up his middle finger.

"That's great!" the cameraman said. "Give me another one!"

"You want me to give you both fingers?" Loco snickered. Malevolent shook his head at his friend's sarcasm as Portia couldn't help but laugh at Loco joking around.

The men took the next photo seriously, glaring directly into the camera's lens. From Malevolent's glare, he wanted his audience to feel his pain and relate to him, all while enjoying the fun music he created. He knew that to have a long-lasting career in this cut-throat business, he had to grow; he couldn't keep producing the same dark-toned music over and over again.

"Malevolent probably spent over one hundred thousand," Loco mused as he glared into the camera's lens, but from the corner of his eye, he caught sight of Portia's jewel. "Probably over five thousand or more."

"Beautiful! Beautiful!" the cameraman praised them. Then Malevolent and Loco leaned back in their chairs, staring at the camera without a care in the world. Portia stood in the background, observing the mini photo session. For a moment, Portia felt like she was backstage at one of her boyfriend's concerts. During this time, Portia noticed Loco glaring at her, which was a bit much. The only thing she could do was keep her eyes focused on Malevolent, but the corner of her eye kept catching Loco's stares, which pierced her body like a butcher knife. The only thing she could do was ignore him.

That night, the muscle car parked before Portia's front door as its brakes screeched and engine rumbled. Portia and Malevolent engaged in a kiss, hoping not to disturb the peace. She glanced at her home, noticing every light was on. Her parents were probably pacing the floor, worried about her getting home late. Malevolent knew that Portia's parents were overprotective and didn't like her coming home at all hours of the night. He couldn't convince Mr. Fairchild that his daughter was in good hands. No father trusts his daughter's so-called boyfriend and would hit the ceiling when he saw that ring. All Malevolent knew was to keep the faith.

"Baby, I've got some business to take care of, and I'll see you when I see you," Malevolent said.

"Okay. Likewise," Portia replied, kissing Malevolent on the cheek.

"That's all I get?" Malevolent raised an eyebrow. Then the two lovers kissed passionately.

"Good night, Mal," Portia said as she exited the passenger seat, closing the door behind her.

"Good night," Malevolent responded as he watched her dash to the front door. As Portia entered, her father's shadow glared at him. All Mr. Fairchild did was stand there like an ominous figure from some eerie place, warning him to be cautious with his daughter, especially if he was serious about wanting to spend the rest of his life with her. Malevolent refused to let this man's presence instill fear in his heart. Then the muscle car sped off with its monstrous engine roaring.

Later that same night, glistening candles and tiny fairy lights illuminated a fancy restaurant as servers attended to the guests. Soothing elevator music played from the ceiling, and New York City décor plastered on the walls gave the ambience of the Big Apple. Sitting alone at a booth, Loco stared at the bright candlelight, his bubbly beer in a tall glass failing to capture his attention. Something about that candle brought him back to a time long ago when he heard the whistling wind as goosebumps surfaced on his neck from the frigid air.

On a somber winter day several years earlier, light snow blanketed the parking lot of Queens College. The campus presented its annual holiday concert in the Kupferberg Auditorium. Rap music played at a medium volume from a navy-blue Audi A4 as it halted in a parking space. The music subsided along with the car's engine, and Loco exited the driver's seat, putting on his jacket while scanning the campus with his eyes. The cold air pierced his face like tiny needles, and he wished he had brought a hat—he knew he would catch a cold. But being pigheaded, Loco disregarded the thought. He saw concertgoers dressed as if they were going to Lincoln Center, wearing dresses, three-piece suits, and long winter coats. His frosted breath hit his face, reminding him again that he should have worn a hat. He had none, and he never did, even in the coldest weather. He caught colds but never bothered to wear one. Satisfied with his nice jacket, he slammed the driver's door and swaggered into the concert hall.

"Winter" by Vivaldi played from a small orchestra of fifteen musicians—cellists, violinists, and a pianist. Zadie played her violin among her peers, garbed in a black gown with a gray bow. She looked stunning in the fabulous gown that Loco had financed. Loco seated himself in the third row, center, smiling at his beautiful violinist as she drew her bow across the strings of her instrument. This was Loco's fourth time attending Zadie's Christmas recital; he never stayed backstage because he couldn't get a good look at her, only a side view. Her parents, Mr. and Mrs. Veico, sat beside him, enjoying a perfect view of their daughter. The audience erupted in applause as the orchestra concluded the classical piece.

The spotlight dimmed, creating a gloomy starry video background on stage. Loco leaned forward in his seat, fully aware this was the moment. A somber solo violin screeched throughout the auditorium. Zadie stood poised on stage, drawing her bow along the strings of her violin. The black gown draped around her slim body fit her beautifully. Loco couldn't stop smiling; that was his girl, performing for all to see. He leaned in his seat, enjoying her show. She always played tunes for him and for local hip-hop artists, but he loved when Zadie performed her own style of music. He never told her what to play or how to play it, allowing this musical genius to add her touches to anything she collaborated on.

As Zadie drew her bow on her violin and slowed down, it sounded as if she were playing a tune for someone's funeral. Was someone going to die? Or had someone already died?

While Zadie continued with her solo performance, Loco glanced at her parents, noticing tears in her mother's eyes. Mrs. Veico's joyful droplets reflected her pride, while her father was visibly choked up—after all, their daughter was a genius. Zadie had a way of evoking strong emotions in everyone who listened. Loco attempted to fight his tears, but a single droplet trickled down his cheek. He wiped it away, shutting his eyes to suppress further tears. Then, there was a thud against the enormous wooden stage. Loco opened his eyes. The audience rose to their feet, screaming, "Zadie!" Mrs. Veico exclaimed.

Zadie collapsed, violin still in hand, on stage. Her colleagues, teacher, and the show's director rushed to her aid. Loco sprang from his seat, pushing his way through the crowd to reach the stage.

"Zadie! Zadie, baby!" Loco called, cradling her in his arms, holding her hand.

Zadie lay unresponsive and lifeless, not feeling the kisses from her boyfriend's lips on her hand. She always loved the way he kissed her hand, and he kept doing it, hoping she would come back to him. "Zadie, answer me, baby," Loco sniffled, his eyes watering.

"Loco! Loco!" a voice echoed, calling his name. He snapped out of his trance, returning to the present. His vision was blurry with tears streaming down his face. Loco wiped them away, trying to fend off more watery droplet memories of his deceased girlfriend. As his vision cleared, his eyes remained red and puffy.

"Are you okay, Loco?" Benji asked, patting him on the shoulder.

"Yeah. I'm cool," Loco sniffled, grimacing.

"What happened? What's bothering you?" Benji pressed, meeting his gaze. He snapped his fingers, beckoning the server.

"Yes, sir. Are you gentlemen ready to order?" the server smiled, holding a computerized tablet.

"No, not yet. Can you bring a glass of water?" Benji insisted.

"Yes, sir," the server hurried away from their booth.

"What's going on?" Benji leaned in toward Loco.

"I'm just thinking about Zadie," Loco admitted, getting choked up.

"I'm sorry, man," Benji exhaled.

"Portia reminds me so much of Zadie. They're both beautiful, musically talented, and sweethearts. I was hoping that Portia and I would be an item, but Malevolent's got her. Fuck!" Loco slammed his fist on the table.

"There are plenty of women in the world, Loco. What about Jazzy?" Benji suggested.

"No. She's used up. I can't even have sex with her right," Loco sneered.

"I thought a man like you could handle that," Benji snickered.

"Shit! You need ten men to handle her. Jazzy's ass is so huge. That fuckin' BBL," Loco shook his head in shame.

"Don't worry; Mrs. Right will be right around the corner," Benji reassured him, bumping fists.

"Miss Right is right in front of me," Loco retorted, staring intently at Benji.

"Are you serious about Portia?" Benji asked, raising an eyebrow and frowning.

"Fuck yeah," Loco replied.

Just then, the servers approached their booth, placing two glasses of water on the table. "Are you gentlemen ready yet?"

"Not yet. I'll let you know," Benji said, and the server scurried away.

"Loco, you can't do that," Benji reiterated.

"Who says I can't? I'm going to get Portia," Loco declared with a smile.

"You can't take her. Are you serious?" Benji leaned back in his seat, then leaned forward again.

"If not that, then what?" Loco shrugged.

"Find someone else!" Benji's eyes widened.

"What's up!" Malevolent swaggered to the booth and took a seat facing his best friend. Malevolent and Loco locked eyes, glaring at one another for a minute.

"What's up, Loco?" Malevolent asked, his tone sharp.

"You tell me. Shit," Loco cursed.

"What the fuck do you mean, shit? What's the problem?" Malevolent pressed.

"Let's chill. We've got business to take care of," Benji tried to defuse the tension.

"Where is this coming from?" Malevolent demanded, focusing his eyes elsewhere.

Again, Benji beckoned the server. "Are you ready to order now, sir?"

"Bring me a beer. Do you want a beer, Mal?" Benji snapped his fingers.

"Yeah, whatever," Malevolent replied, refusing to make eye contact with his best friend. He wondered, *"What got into Loco? Why is he so ticked off?"*

"Bring two beers, another water, and salad for all of us. For now," Benji ordered. The server typed it into their computerized tablet.

"I don't eat salad," Malevolent sneered at Benji.

"Whatever. There's a first time for everything. Thank you," Benji said as the server scurried away.

Benji took a deep breath, his eyes shifting from side to side as he focused on the hip-hop duo. He tried to ignore the earlier tension and aimed for the future. Benji and Loco shifted their focus to releasing Malevolent's first track to the public, "Machete."

Malevolent nodded in agreement, eager to know what else needed to be done. Loco added his input into their success, and for now, they acted as if everything were normal. They both knew something was off but had to stay focused on their dream. Benji joined the conversation just as the server brought their order.

CHAPTER FOURTEEN

Red neon lights illuminated in Malevolent's living room apartment, preventing it from plunging into darkness. An enormous Coqui frog canvas hung on the wall, a tall lamp, a sofa, recliner, a flat panel television and an old desktop computer made this set up perfect for a bachelor. Keys rattled, and the front door's lock clicked as Malevolent aggressively pushed the door open. He stormed in, slamming the door so hard that it shook the entire building. He didn't care if it disturbed the other tenants; his mind was elsewhere. Tossing his keys onto the coffee table, he plummeted onto the couch, leaving his shoes and clothes on. Glaring at the ceiling, he thought about the tension between him and Loco when they were teens. Speaking of Portia, he grabbed his cellphone and dialed her number. The call connected, but it rang and rang without her picking up. Malevolent disconnected the call, figuring she was probably asleep. Luckily, he was off from work that night, so he had some time to himself. He reminisced about the summer when he and Loco almost lost their friendship over some bullshit. Closing his eyes, he couldn't shake off the echoes of yelling and cursing that haunted his mind.

Low humidity and a temperature of eighty-seven made this summer day pleasant for those who preferred a comfortable feel. Eighteen-year-old Alejandro slumped over on a bar stool in his garage, cluttered with old paintings, chairs, records, clothes, and three old bikes. Tools decorated the brick walls like a museum, featuring a saw, hammer, machete, and other gardening equipment. He stood up and swaggered to the sidewalk, pacing back and forth. His racing heart thumped as sweat began to form on his forehead, which he wiped away with his hand. Brakes screeched as a gray Cherokee Jeep swerved around the corner. Alejandro's face turned red as he balled up his fists and gritted his teeth. "Here's this motherfucker right now! I'm ready!"

The vehicle's brakes screeched and halted at the curb just before Alejandro. Rap music blasted from inside as Loco jumped from the driver's seat. The two young men began dancing around in a circle like boxers, ready to fight, fists raised but wordlessly attempting to avoid a physical altercation.

"I fuckin' paid almost a thousand dollars for my session!" Malevolent swung a punch at Loco's face but missed.

"You missed, bitch!" Loco guffawed, keeping his fists up.

"I didn't complete my session, so give me half of the money back!" Malevolent then punched Lorenzo in the face.

"Got your ass, motherfucker! Where's my shit?" Malevolent noticed a stream of blood trickling from Loco's nose.

Loco felt the warmth and moisture on his face and touched it, noticing the blood on his fingers. He then threw the money in Alejandro's face—cash consisting of twenties, fifties, and hundreds flying everywhere on the sidewalk. Loco returned with a punch to Alejandro's face, causing blood to surface. The two wrestled on the concrete in the middle of the street, drawing attention from an oncoming vehicle that slowed down, honking, while neighbors watched the chaotic scene.

"What the hell, Alejandro!" Erasmo stormed through the front door to break up the fight.

"That's right! I checked that face!" Loco guffawed.

"And look at the bloody mess on you, ass!" Malevolent tried to punch Lorenzo again, but his grandfather restrained him.

"Shut up!" Erasmo smacked Alejandro on the head a couple of times. "What the hell are you two fighting about?" He noticed the cash scattered on the ground.

"He needed his money back for a session that wasn't completed, and he kept refusing to give it to me," Alejandro gathering his cash.

"I told you there were other acts in the studio!" Lorenzo argued, moving to get in Alejandro's face. Erasmo stepped in to separate the two.

"Let's calm down, Lorenzo!"

"You should've given me my money sooner, or did you spend it on someone?" Alejandro, Lorenzo, and Erasmo eyed Zadie, who was in the passenger seat. She shrank back, realizing all eyes were on her.

"Don't say shit about my girl!" Lorenzo confronted his best friend.

"Yo, Zadie! Look at your man's fucked-up face!" Alejandro teased.

"Get in the damn house, Alejandro! Now!" Erasmo pointed toward the front door of their home. Alejandro chuckled as he swaggered inside.

"Are you alright, Lorenzo?" Erasmo patted him on the shoulder.

"I've got a lot of respect for you, Mr. Valasquez," Lorenzo said, turning red. His heart raced, and he slowed his breathing.

"I love you like another son. You and Alejandro grew up together. This isn't like you two. What the hell is this about? Money!" Erasmo asked. As soon as he asked that question, Lorenzo's eyes fell on Zadie in the passenger seat. Erasmo raised an eyebrow and shook his head because it couldn't be true.

"Please go home and take care of yourself. I'm going to talk to Alejandro, okay?" Erasmo embraced Lorenzo. "Are you cool?"

"Yes, I'll be alright," Lorenzo said abruptly, releasing himself from Erasmo's embrace and hopping back into the driver's seat of his car. He sped off.

Minutes later, rap music blared from Alejandro's bedroom as Erasmo pounded on the door. "Alejandro, open up!"

"I'm busy, Pop!" Alejandro shouted.

Erasmo stood for a moment, lifting his hand to pound on the door again. He didn't want to upset his grandson further, but he had embarrassed their family in front of the entire neighborhood. Erasmo didn't care about his grandson's privacy.

"Open up! Open up! Open up!" Erasmo knocked persistently on Alejandro's bedroom door.

Martha stepped into the hallway from their master bedroom, wiping her eyes. "What's the problem, Erasmo?"

"Alejandro and Lorenzo were fighting!" Erasmo hollered.

"Fighting?" Martha raised an eyebrow.

"Didn't you hear them?" Erasmo waved his arms in the air.

"I had my headphones on," Martha replied.

"If I hadn't broken those two up, our grandson would be in

jail or worse!" Erasmo continued pounding on the door. Just then, Alejandro swung the bedroom door open.

"Stop banging on my door; you're giving me a headache!"

Erasmo barged into Alejandro's bedroom and turned off the radio, glaring at his own flesh and blood and the large sum of cash strewn across his computer desk. Alejandro didn't bother to count it; instead, he waited for his grandfather to speak. "Was he going to kick him out? Or what?" Alejandro wondered, lounging in his recliner, still gazing at his grandfather. Erasmo exhaled, noticing Martha standing in the doorway. He beckoned her to step aside for a man-to-man talk. Martha stepped away, shaking her head in disappointment as Erasmo took slow steps toward his grandson, sitting on the edge of his bed.

"What's gotten into you, Alejandro? And what's with all this money here?"

"Lorenzo promised to give me back my money for an incomplete session," Alejandro replied, counting the bills in his hand.

"So, what happened?" Erasmo asked.

"He almost took my money and ran, so I confronted him," Alejandro continued counting. "I think I'm short two hundred dollars!"

"Don't worry about that right now," Erasmo sighed.

"Don't worry? What do you mean, Pop! Don't worry!" Alejandro exploded.

"I'll give you the two hundred dollars back!" his grandfather said.

"No! Lorenzo is going to give me back my cash!" Alejandro pounded his fist on the desk.

"Don't go and do anything stupid, Alejandro! You've embarrassed yourself enough by wrestling in the street right before the whole world's eyes!" his grandfather exclaimed.

"I won't!" Alejandro said defiantly.

"I hope not! And I hope this isn't over Zadie. Is... it?" Erasmo glared at him.

Alejandro diverted his gaze, seeing the intensity in his grandfather's eyes as he demanded an answer. Inhaling deeply, Alejandro made eye contact and shrugged.

"Maybe?"

"Please don't end up like your father!" Erasmo warned.

"You won't have to worry, Pop. If I ever have a tug-of-war over a girl again, there won't be any unaliving of self. I'll fight to the death," Alejandro smirked.

"No fighting, period!" Erasmo stomped his foot on the floor.

"That's what men do!" Alejandro retorted.

Just then, the doorbell rang.

"I'll get that!" Alejandro said, exiting his bedroom.

Seconds later, Alejandro swaggered to the front door and swung it open. Muffled voices emanated from radios on the hips of three police officers standing on the porch. As police sirens echoed throughout the neighborhood, Alejandro's heart raced. He knew he had to explain what had occurred earlier but didn't want to snitch on his best friend. So, he had to lie. His grandfather rushed to the door, attempting to explain to the officers that everything was under control. It was just boys being boys; chances are they would patch things up later.

An hour later, Alejandro woke up from a short nap, stretching and yawning. He grabbed his cellphone and noticed a text from Portia, along with a voicemail. It read:

> Hello Babe, I hope to see you tomorrow. I'm getting ready to go to sleep and I'll call You in the morning. Good night.

Alejandro quickly typed a response, then laid his phone on the table and closed his eyes. He stretched out on his sofa and tried to catch some more sleep. He wanted to go to bed because it was more comfortable. He closed his eyes, not thinking about the short dream he had of his past. Yes, he and Loco had fought over music and over Zadie. He wished it hadn't happened because now history seemed to be repeating itself. He then erased the dream from his mind and dozed off.

Clad in a superhero t-shirt, jeans, and red socks, seven-year-old Alejandro lounged in bed, watching Saturday morning cartoons. His small bedroom had blue-painted walls, adorned with posters of his favorite cartoon characters and superheroes, filled wall to wall with toys. No one could navigate through this self-made toy store that Alejandro pretended to create. Laughter erupted from the kitchen, drowning out the sounds of his cartoon shows.

Alejandro rose from his slumber to turn down the volume on the TV, hearing more laughter once again.

"Papi!" Alejandro's eyes widened as he sprang from his bed. He dashed into the kitchen and halted in his tracks. He witnessed his mother and a strange man kissing, their affection escalating. Alejandro didn't recognize this man; he was not his father. His mother and this "Rico Suave" guy were intertwined—mouth to mouth, cheek to cheek, breath to breath, heart to heart, pelvis to pelvis—while she had her thighs wrapped around his waist. Alejandro's mother seemed to enjoy being in this stranger's arms, doing things a child should not see.

As he watched, a fiery red hue rose to Alejandro's face. He stomped his foot on the floor. “Where's my father?”

"I'm right here, Papi!" his father stepped into the kitchen through the side door. Alejandro gasped, noticing his father approaching Rosa and her lover as they were about to strip down completely.

Edgar stared at them, hands balled into fists. Alejandro could feel his father's rage. He wished his father would punch this guy in the face but not do anything to his mother; he wanted to give her the benefit of the doubt. “Who are you?” Edgar approached the young interloper.

“Claudio!” the arrogant young man responded, sticking out his chest as if ready for confrontation.

“Claudio who?” Edgar shouted, throwing his arms in the air.

“Don’t worry about who the fuck I am!” Claudio smirked, stepping closer to Edgar’s face.

“You’re fucking my wife!” Edgar exploded, wrapping an arm around Claudio’s neck and wrestling him to the floor. Rosa tried to break them apart but couldn’t stop the chaos. Alejandro rushed to pull his mother away from the fight, fearing she would suffer consequences.

"Mom, let's go! Please!" Alejandro pleaded, tugging on her arm.

"Go to your room, Alejandro!" Rosa ordered, pushing her son away while keeping her focus on the men.

Young Alejandro persisted, attempting to pull his mother away from the chaos.

"I said go to your room!" Rosa shoved Alejandro so hard that he hit the wall. THUD. Luckily, he wasn’t hurt, but no one noticed the young child hit the wall.

Neighbors rushed through the side door, drawn to the escalating fight. A female neighbor grabbed Alejandro and carried him to his bedroom, closing the door behind them. The voices of Alejandro's parents' love triangle echoed in his head, causing a cacophony of confusion.

Malevolent woke up on the couch again, back in reality. He looked around his living room as sunlight beamed through the windows. He also heard the birds singing; of course, it wasn't time to get to work until later that night. Malevolent swaggered from the living room to his bedroom. Once there, he stripped off his pants, shirt, and shoes, leaving only his boxers on. He hopped into bed and pulled the covers over himself, settling in for some sleep.

CHAPTER FIFTEEN

That afternoon, in the beautiful and quiet Douglaston neighborhood, Loco sped his Jaguar E-Pace through the streets, not caring about other motorists or pedestrians in sight. He steered the wheel with one hand, increasing the volume on his radio. He blasted Malevolent's song "Machete" for some strange reason. Upset with his best friend, he wondered, *"Why am I playing this song?"* He didn't bother to think about his actions. Loco continued driving, hoping no police were patrolling the area, but there were surveillance cameras. He had no choice but to slow down, the brakes of his vehicle squealing at a red traffic light. As he glanced over his shoulder, he spotted a red Toyota, occupied by a glass-clad, polo-shirted guy and a beautiful girl applying makeup in the passenger seat. Loco found the girl stunning but assumed she was probably shallow, incapable of being serious with the corny guy taking her on a first date, likely trying to score by the end of it. Just the thought made him scoff as the traffic light turned green. He then sped off in his Jaguar, leaving a smoky mist from his rear wheels.

Within a matter of minutes, the Jaguar parked in front of a charming blue and white Victorian home with manicured lawns and oak trees. Loco shut down the engine and exited the driver's side, taking his time to analyze the house and the surrounding neighborhood. It was eerily quiet, the only sound being the chirping of birds. He trotted to the front door and rang the doorbell, its haunting chimes echoing. Glancing over his shoulder, he hoped no one would ambush him. The gentle chimes of the bronze wind chime hung above his head, swaying softly. Footsteps hurried from inside, and the door swung open. Loco's face lit up with a grin. "How are you doing, Portia?"

"Hi," Portia responded, her jaw dropping. "Loco, what are you doing here?"

"I came to see how you're doing," Loco said, embracing her small-framed body. He showered her with kisses, attempting to inch closer to her lips. Portia pushed him away.

"I'm fine," she replied, shifting her eyes left and right, hoping Malevolent wasn't around.

"I missed you at the studio," he rubbed her back. Portia politely pushed his hands away.

"Don't you have a girlfriend?" she asked.

"No," Loco lied through his teeth.

"What happened to Jazzy?" she asked, a smirk creeping onto her face.

"Jazzy and I aren't cutting it. She's not...," before Loco could finish his sentence, Mrs. Fairchild marched to the front door.

"Alejandro?" she cried, arching an eyebrow at the stranger standing on her doorstep. She realized this wasn't her daughter's boyfriend.

"Hello, Mrs. Fairchild." Loco shook Portia's mother's hand.

Her mother giggled like a schoolgirl encountering a handsome young man trying to capture her daughter's heart.

"And you are?" she leaned in to get a better look at him.

"I'm Loco, but you can call me Lorenzo," he added.

"Lorenzo. That's nice. Are you a friend of Alejandro's?" Portia's mother asked.

"Yes, I am. We're best friends, in fact. We've known each other since high school," Loco continued his life story. Portia didn't like the idea of him coming to her home. *"What the hell was he doing? If Malevolent finds out, it'll be hell,"* she thought. Just then, Portia's father marched to the front door, noticing the stranger, arching his eyebrow. For some strange reason, without any bad vibes, Mr. Fairchild shook Loco's hand and invited him to dinner. Portia's eyes widened; she couldn't believe her father was entertaining her boyfriend's best friend. She wanted to curse Loco out and chase him away, but she had to keep her cool. Malevolent was going to be furious when he heard this.

At dinner, Portia, Loco, and her parents gathered around the dining room table for another Sunday meal of roasted chicken, rice, potatoes, and veggies. Mr. Fairchild resided at the head of the table, devouring his dinner while chatting with his new guest. Mrs. Fairchild sat at the other end, listening and laughing with her husband and his new best friend. Portia absorbed it all, feeling overshadowed. Her father treated Loco with more respect than Malevolent. Was it because Loco had connections in the music industry and rubbed elbows with big-name artists? She could tell her father preferred Loco for her than Malevolent, and her mother would probably agree.

"Malevolent and I go way back to high school," Loco laughed, shoving a spoonful of veggies into his mouth.

"That's wonderful, and you two are going to be very successful," Mrs. Fairchild clapped her hands, thrilled. She loved seeing Portia bring home accomplished men and not some loser. Portia attempted to leave the table but didn't want to disrespect her parents; she never displayed rude behavior toward them. So, she rolled with the punches, wondering about Loco's family. *Did he come from a dysfunctional home? Had he ever been locked up?* Just by looking at his entourage, it said a lot.

"Malevolent is my best friend, and we've had fallouts, but we always patched things up," Loco snickered.

"What types of fallouts?" Mr. Fairchild asked.

"Money and... women," Loco winked at Portia.

"Excuse me, I forgot something in the kitchen," Portia excused herself from the table, storming into the kitchen.

Within a few minutes, Portia placed the cover on the roaster of chicken, attempting to store it in the refrigerator. She tapped the side of the roaster, noticing it was still hot. She placed the bird back on the island with the rest of the spread. Portia eyed the food; she could've easily stashed the veggies, rice, potatoes, and salad away, but instead, she slouched in an iron chair. She had no other choice but to leave everything intact, the way her mother prepared it. Her mother always created beautiful three-course meals for holidays and special occasions. Portia lingered in the iron chair, fixed herself a small plate of food, and enjoyed her own company. She felt it was her obligation to tell Malevolent, but she didn't want anything terrible to happen. Loco had admitted to her parents that he and Malevolent had differences in the past over money and women, then winked at her. Portia knew she could be caught in the middle of some serious issues. She shoved a piece of chicken into her mouth, her eyes watering. A tear streamed down her cheek, which she quickly wiped away.

"Portia! What are you doing?" Mrs. Fairchild marched in with her hands on her hips.

Portia held back further tears and faced her mother, faking a smile. Her mother noticed something was wrong. "Are you okay?"

"No!" Portia shook her head, flashing the ring before her mother's eyes.

"That's beautiful. Who gave you that?" Mrs. Fairchild pointed toward the dining room.

"No!" Portia waved her arms in the air.

"Alejandro?" Mrs. Fairchild whispered.

"Yes, he means so much to me. Do you like Alejandro?" Portia sighed.

"Yes, Alejandro is a fine young man, and so is Lorenzo," Mrs. Fairchild said.

Portia glared at her mother, dismayed by her answer. She wanted her mother to dismiss Lorenzo, but it was Portia's job to do that. Right about now, Alejandro was likely sleeping because he had to work the night shift, but he was probably going to stop by before heading to work. She could hear Loco and her father enjoying their conversation like old friends. But she had to send Loco on his way before Malevolent showed up.

In no time, Portia and Loco lounged on the loveseat patio furniture in her expansive backyard, surrounded by trees, bushes, flowers, and other plants that created a paradise setting for anyone, especially lovers. It was quiet. Loco couldn't keep his eyes off Portia while she focused elsewhere. "Why are you quiet, Portia?" he nudged her.

"I have nothing to say," Portia replied, still avoiding eye contact.

"Portia. Portia, look at me." Loco lifted her chin so her eyes could focus on him. He then leaned in for a kiss.

"Please leave, Loco!" Portia jumped from her seat before his lips met hers. Loco rose to his feet and approached her. "I'm sorry, Portia. I didn't mean any disrespect."

"You are being disrespectful—not just toward me, but toward Alejandro," Portia folded her arms.

"I'm going to let you know something: you remind me of someone who was very dear to me," Loco said, his voice quivering as tears welled in his eyes. A single tear cascaded down his face, which he quickly wiped away.

"I'm sorry for your loss," Portia said, stepping back.

"My girl Zadie played the violin beautifully and was a local celebrity. When I first laid eyes on her, I had to have her. We were together for several years, and she helped me create music for some local rappers. Then one day... she slipped away." Loco proceeded to fight back more tears.

Portia's eyes watered, feeling his pain.

"Did Malevolent mention Zadie?"

"No. Why should he?"

"Because he and Zadie were supposed to be together," Loco responded.

"Okay. What are you trying to say?" Portia asked.

"Like I said earlier, when Malevolent and I were younger, we fought over a lot of things." Loco inched toward Portia and gently kissed her on the cheek before stepping away.

Portia's eyes brimmed with tears, stomping into the house, slamming the door.

Later that evening, Portia flashed the ring before her father's eyes while lounging in his recliner in the living room. Mr. Fairchild's eyes nearly popped out of their sockets at the sight of the glittering diamond on his daughter's finger. He glared at Portia, hoping Alejandro truly loved her. Abruptly, he grabbed the television remote and turned on the TV. Portia sensed that her father wasn't impressed, but her mother embraced her, keeping the faith. Mr. Fairchild offered no acknowledgment of her presence, making Portia feel as if she were being punished for bringing home a guy without enough status. Yet, she believed Alejandro was going to make something of himself. But her father didn't see it that way. Portia raced upstairs, sobbing. Mrs. Fairchild glared at her husband, shaking her head, then waltzed into the kitchen.

Within seconds, Portia flung the bedroom door open and slammed it hard. The loud noise shook the entire house, and she didn't care if her father lectured her about being childish. She stared at the door, waiting for her parents to confront her about the shaking. Chances were Malevolent would stop by to see her before he headed to work. Portia put her ear close to her door, trying to hear if her parents were coming up the stairs. Nothing. She only heard the television blaring from the living room, the volume increasing. Her father did that to drown out her tantrums, something she had never done before. "What got into her father?" Portia wondered. It was probably because he wanted grandchildren before his time was up on this earth. But this wasn't about her father's wants; it was about what she wanted. Her happiness mattered. Her parents already lived their lives with her as an addition; now it was her turn.

Just then, her cellphone vibrated on the nightstand. She grabbed it and saw a text message from Alejandro: *I'm on my way.* Her heart raced as she peered out of her bedroom window, hoping to see that Dodge Challenger speeding toward her home. She couldn't hear the engine yet; Alejandro wasn't close enough to hear his SRT engine in the distance. Hurriedly, she dashed down the stairs, breezing past her father, whose head was glued to the loud television. Portia looked out of the living room window, but the blasting TV muffled the sound of Alejandro's arrival.

"Shit!" Portia muttered.

Then she heard the thunderous roar of the muscle car in the distance. She flung open the front door just as Alejandro's car stopped short at the curb. Portia dashed out as Alejandro exited the driver's side with the engine still running. The two rushed into each other's arms as if they hadn't seen one another in years. When two people are in love, that's how it feels. They kissed passionately, wrapped in each other's embrace. Portia felt Alejandro's strength in his hold; she knew he loved her, and she loved him in return.

As Portia opened her eyes, she noticed her mother watching them. Mrs. Fairchild's jaw dropped, unable to believe how in love her daughter and the aspiring rapper were. She glanced over her shoulder to see if her husband was coming to the window, but he didn't. Portia's mother proceeded to observe the couple, as if watching a love story unfold right before her eyes. She even eavesdropped on their dialogue.

"How are you, babe?" Portia kissed Alejandro on the cheek.

"I'm tired. I can't wait until I resign," Alejandro yawned.

"And then you'll live the good life and won't have to worry about anyone telling you what to do," Portia chuckled.

"Really? I still have to answer to someone," he replied, stroking Portia's cheeks.

"I'll make a plate for you," she said, taking Alejandro's hand and escorting him inside.

Before long, Portia and Alejandro sat at the dining room table, eating the Sunday dinner that had been prepared earlier.

Even Loco had taken part in enjoying the meal, trying to charm Portia while Alejandro had been away. She wanted to tell Alejandro about everything, but she allowed him to eat in peace, noticing how he shoved the chicken into his mouth, clearly starving. If they were to tie the knot, he would have to worry about food. On the contrary, she might just feed him too much. Portia ate a smaller portion while Alejandro devoured a larger one. After gulping down his soda, Alejandro burped.

"Excuse me. Did you make this?" he asked, glancing at Portia.

"Yes, I did," she smiled.

"You're a good cook," he complimented, pinching her cheeks.

"Thank you. You should come over on Thanksgiving," Portia said.

"I look forward to it. Hopefully, if I don't go on tour or anything because this business moves fast," he paused, glaring at Portia.

"Did your parents see the ring?" Alejandro asked as he continued eating.

"Yes, they saw it," Portia sipped her soda. Alejandro looked at her, waiting for more information.

"And?" he pressed.

"They're happy," she told a half-truth.

"I can tell your father doesn't like me. And that's okay," Alejandro said, shoving another spoonful of rice into his mouth.

"No, that's not okay. I don't want him disrespecting you," Portia whined.

"There's nothing I can do about it, and not even you," Alejandro shrugged, finishing his dinner. Portia knew he wasn't going to take any disrespect from her father. If he and her father clashed, she would undoubtedly side with Alejandro. Maybe their families should meet over the holidays or some event. Alejandro swallowed his food and sipped his soda, noticing that Portia was staring at him.

"Why are you quiet, Portia?" Alejandro asked with his mouth full.

"It's a Sunday evening. It's God's time, so everything and everyone is still," Portia chuckled, shrugging. She saw that Alejandro was almost finished with his meal.

"And you know, Monday through Saturday is the devil's days," Portia continued taking small bites from her plate. Alejandro glared at her—he didn't believe she was religious, but had no issue with his stage name.

"Of course, he dominates those days. Look at the state of the world," Alejandro wiped his mouth with his napkin. Then he burped again. "Excuse me. That was good, baby,"

"Thank you. You're welcome to a meal anytime," Portia said, kissing Alejandro on the cheek as she grabbed their plates and headed to the kitchen.

Minutes later, Malevolent and Portia lingered in his Dodge Challenger parked in front of her residence. He bragged about his album "Mourning Rose" and was excited about it's released, but he still had to produce more songs. He knew Portia didn't want to go to the studio anymore, but still wished to contribute her piano tracks. And she had to figure something out.

"Honey, I can go to the studio in the city and create some more pieces for you," Portia smiled. Malevolent rubbed her cheek and continuously kissed her.

"I don't want you going to the city alone, Portia. That's too dangerous," Malevolent hugged her tightly.

"I'll be okay. My piano teacher is there and some other students," Portia insisted.

"Alright. Where?" Malevolent asked.

"At Penthouse Studios in the city," she replied.

"Loco and I have been there before; that studio is nice. When are you going?" he asked.

"Maybe tomorrow, because I know you have to finish your project," Portia answered.

"You better call me. I'm going to pick you up. I forbid you to ride the trains late at night or take a taxi with a weird driver," Alejandro warned, wagging his finger at her.

"Yes, babe," she replied lovingly.

"I love you," he laid a passionate kiss on Portia. "I'll see you in a couple of days, and get those piano tracks ready for me. I know you can do it," he said, waving his finger at her.

"I promise, Alejandro. I love you too," Portia kissed him.

"I've got to get to work. See you later," Malevolent started up his engine as Portia exited the vehicle. She kept her eyes focused on him, backing up towards her house. She blew a kiss to him and waving. Then the Dodge Challenger blasted off down the street as it honked. Portia then faced forward, marching towards her house. She knew she had to get to the recording studio as soon as possible. Portia wanted to asked Malevolent about Zadie. *"Did Malevolent and Zadie have a relationship? How long were they together? And did he love Zadie and miss her? Or was this Loco's way to ruin Portia and Malevolent's relationship?"* Portia still chose not to say anything to Malevolent because he would suspect something. So, for now, she was going to focus on his music.

CHAPTER SIXTEEN

The next morning at Penthouse Music Studios, Portia sat on a cushioned piano stool at a black piano, surrounded by bright ceiling lights, wooden walls, and a glossed floor. She wore headphones as her fingers danced across the keys. Before her lounged a middle-aged gentleman, Sam, along with three studio engineers seated before a soundboard. The forty-something man, dressed in khaki pants, a polo shirt, and worn sneakers, leaned back and listened intently to the various piano pieces Portia played. He raised an eyebrow and frowned, trying to understand the purpose of this session. He figured that, since she was in the music business, she must be working with someone in the field. Relaxing in his recliner, he proceeded to record.

Portia noticed his body language and considered explaining her musical piece, but she continued to play various tunes, improvising as she went. She wanted to give Alejandro the opportunity to use these piano pieces to create whatever he desired. Portia performed a dark tune that could evoke sadness or anger in anyone who heard it. Alejandro's goal with this album was to delve into a dark place where he could truly be himself. Whatever that self was, she only knew that his parents had a bad breakup that resulted in his father taking his own life. As Portia played, she felt like a star under the spotlight, momentarily forgetting if she wanted to be in the limelight. "What pianist becomes successful without singing? Plenty of them!" she thought.

Suddenly, she played an eerie composition and noticed a figure swaggering into the studio. He shook hands with her piano instructor. Portia's eyes bulged as she recognized Loco. "How the hell did he know where I was?" Her heart raced, and her face turned red. Agitated, she played more aggressively, her fingers pressing down on the keys faster and harder. Anyone could tell she was unhappy. "What does he want?" she said to herself. "Why doesn't he go find Jazzy?"

Loco waved at her from the glass window, dropping into a recliner beside her instructor. She glared at him, feeling as if he owned the place. Unsure of whether to cease the session or continue, her fingers refused to miss a note. She noticed Loco and her music instructor chatting like old friends. *"Do they know each other?"* Finally, she cut the session short, closed the piano lid, and rose from the bench. Snatching off her headphones, she tossed them aside without concern. Portia barged through the glass door where Loco and her music instructor were conversing.

As she approached, Loco and Sam stopped laughing, noticing Portia standing there with her arms crossed. She needed to know what was going on and wasn't pleased.

"How did you find out about this studio?" she asked, her voice quivering.

"Your instructor Sam and I go way back. It's a small world," Loco said, planting a quick kiss on her cheek.

"Too small," Portia shrugged, storming away.

"Portia! Are you finished?" Sam called out, raising an eyebrow.

"Yes! Email me the music ASAP!" Portia's voice echoed as Loco followed her.

On a crowded Manhattan street minutes later, Portia pounded her footsteps against the concrete, though she wasn't wearing heels. She refused to look over her shoulder, yet she could feel Loco trailing behind her. She wished he'd fall flat on his face into the ground. As determined as Loco was, he would still chase after her with a bloody face—that was disgusting. Looming in front of her, Loco at six foot-two, towered over her while blocking her path. Portia wanted so badly to slap the hell out of Loco. "What the hell is wrong with you!" Her shouting drew the attention of pedestrians walking by.

"Why are you causing a scene, Portia?" Loco replied, grinding his teeth.

"Because... you're bothering me," Portia said, her voice quivering as tears cascaded down her cheeks.

"Why are you crying?" Loco asked, this time in a softer tone.

"Leave me alone! Why are you trying to come between me and Malevolent?" she stomped her foot.

"You're the one... for me," Lorenzo insisted.

"You're full of shit!" Portia threw her arms in the air.

"We can make beautiful music together," Loco said, stepping closer.

"I've got to catch my bus!" Portia attempted to stomp away, but Loco grabbed her arm and laid a kiss on her. He then embraced her tightly, glaring into her eyes.

"Let go of me," Portia pleaded.

"Stop trying to be a good girl. I know you've got a wild side. How many times did Malevolent hit that?" he whispered in her ear, glancing down at her backside.

"That's none of your business!" Portia wept. Passersby noticed her distress.

"You wouldn't want Malevolent to find out that you invited me to your house for dinner and that I met your family," he whispered.

"You invited yourself! And I'm going to tell Alejandro everything!" Portia continued to cry.

"Why would you ruin things for the man you love? Right?" Loco said, sticking his tongue in her ear.

"Stop!" Portia sobbed uncontrollably.

Then, several police cars pulled up to the scene. Loco immediately released Portia from his grasp.

"Ma'am, are you okay?" a police officer asked while several officers surrounded Lorenzo, who threw his hands in the air.

"What's the problem, officer?" he asked, feigning innocence.

"You tell me," a female officer replied, reversing the question.

A team of police officers surrounded Portia as if she were at a news conference, bombarded with inquiries. A migraine crept its way to the left side of her head, shifting to the center, as if someone had hammered a large nail into her skull. Her vision blurred and things began to spin. Portia's body weakened, and she plummeted to the concrete. The officers quickly got on their radios, alerting for help. Loco's jaw dropped while held him in the background.

In a hospital waiting room, Loco paced the slightly damp, ammonia-scented floor while a janitor mopped a few feet away. He hoped Portia would be okay. He was pretty sure she didn't have a heart condition, cancer, or any other undisclosed illnesses—physical or mental—she might know of. Loco recalled when Zadie had kept her illness a secret before she passed. He sat down for a moment but stood right back up as a thin gentleman headed toward him. "Mr. Porter?"

"Yes, what's up, doctor?" Loco answered, fear evident in his eyes.

"Portia's awake. She had a panic attack," the doctor held a medical chart in his hands.

"Can I see her?" Loco glanced over his shoulder.

"Yes, you may," the doctor replied, leading Loco into a hospital room.

In the corner of the room, a television played, illuminating Portia's face as she watched the local news. She rested her arm behind her head, wearing a medical wrist band, medical gown and a blanket covering half of her body. Portia looked around, realizing she was alone and scared. She needed strength if she was going to get home. Worrying about Malevolent finding out about her fainting incident on a busy Manhattan sidewalk made her anxious. Just thinking about it, Portia sat up in her bed, scanning the room, and noticing Loco. He swaggered to her bedside with open arms. "Baby, I'm so sorry," Loco planted a kiss on her cheek.

"My head is killing me," Portia said, taking sharp breaths.

"Take it easy, baby. Do you want some water?" Loco asked, noticing the bottled water and opening it. Portia took a sip and lay back in bed, handing the bottle back to Loco.

"Do you really care about me? Or do you just want me for one thing?" Portia quivered.

"I do care about you, Portia," Loco confidently, puffing out his chest.

She didn't ask him any more questions; Portia didn't know what to believe. All she wanted right now was for Malevolent to be there. She loved him more than anything else in this world, and that's why she wore the ring on her finger so proudly.

"What could Loco possibly do to win Portia over? He couldn't envision himself at Portia and Malevolent's wedding, living happily ever after. Loco wanted to be happy again, and the woman lying in this hospital bed was his wish. Thank God she was okay, and tomorrow she'd likely be released from the hospital. Just then, Mr. and Mrs. Fairchild stormed through the wooden swinging door, dashing to their daughter's bedside. Portia's mother kissed her on the forehead. Mr. Fairchild turned to Loco, shook his hand, and nodded. Loco faded into the background as Portia's parents showered her with hugs and kisses. He felt like a mere spectator in a lifetime drama. He swaggered out of the hospital room, not looking back. He hoped Portia would call out his name, but she didn't. As Loco dragged his construction boots along the shiny tile floor, his vision became blurry. Not another scene of the tearful man. If anyone in the music industry found out he cried over a woman, he would be made fun of. But, wouldn't anyone shed tears over a loved one buried six feet under? It's only human. Loco was human, but he had a dark side—his ambition to acquire as much money as possible and surround himself with cars, clothes, and even the woman he desired. The woman, not women. That's what most artists in this industry desire: women. And that's why they have so many problems. He navigated through doctors, nurses, visitors, patients, and even security guards. He rushed out of the automatic double doors and swaggered through the parking

lot. Wiping his tears, he inserted the keys into his driver's side door and climbed in. He slammed the door shut, sobbing. This big tough guy was a softie...and he felt guilty for putting Portia in harm's way. He knew Malevolent would soon find out, and all hell would break loose. *"And hell, it will be."* Loco revved the engine of his car and sped out of the parking lot.

CHAPTER SEVENTEEN

Red neon lights beamed through Malevolent's master bedroom while he slumbered in his king-sized bed. His black bedsheets wrapped around his waist and halfway up to his abdominal area, crossing over his shoulder just like Christ who rose from the dead, entering into heaven. He slowly opened his eyes, getting his first glimpse at the ceiling—or God—hovering over him. Malevolent believed that his father hopefully was in a beautiful marble palace in heaven. Or maybe he wasn't. He didn't mean to have negative thoughts because he didn't want to wind up in hell. He wasn't sure if he and Loco were going to become a successful rap duo. There seemed to be tension between them, and it could spiral out of control. He hoped they could get this album done successfully without any issues. So far, he had five tracks on the album, and hopefully one of his singles would hit the airwaves. Loco should've had one of his singles out already; he was too busy acting stupid. Hopefully, when they go on tour, dozens of women would drop their panties for Loco and probably then he would forget about Portia. But those same women would do the same for Malevolent. He would never cheat on Portia and would take her on tour with him to avoid screwing up their relationship. For now, he had to think about those piano tracks she was supposed to email him. Malevolent grabbed his cellphone from his nightstand as he sat up in bed. He noticed a text message on his screen and opened it. The message read:

> Hello Malevolent, Here are the piano tracks that I created. I hope there's enough coverage for your album. - Portia

At the bottom of the text were the links to the music tracks. Malevolent noticed there were more than three piano tracks. Murmuring to himself, Malevolent counted the tracks as an even bigger smile surfaced on his face: fourteen piano tracks! He couldn't wait to listen to them and get them to Benji. He noticed that Portia's message was short but not sweet. What was going on with her? Malevolent dialed her phone number, placing the receiver to his ear. There was a connection, but it kept ringing and ringing. No answer. The only thing he could do was leave a message. Then a BEEP.

"Portia, baby! How are you? I haven't seen you, nor have I heard from you. I got the piano tracks you sent me. Thank you. I'll see you later. Love you." Malevolent ended his call. He tossed his cellphone on the bed and marched over to his desk. He lounged in his recliner at his desk, turning on the lamp and opening his laptop. He opened the email Portia sent him, playing the first piano track, which had eerie undertones. He listened for a moment as the black and white keys pleased his ears. Malevolent smiled and then played the second track. Again, another beautiful track satisfied his ears. He rocked in his recliner and knew he couldn't sit there and listen because he had to get to work. So, Malevolent played the piano tracks from his stereo speakers. He turned up the volume while he got ready for work.

Steaming hot water torrented from the showerhead while Malevolent lathered his body with the soapy shower gel. His body resembled a snowman from head to toe as he was deep in thought about each and every key that Portia created. Yes, during his shower, even with the water running—which could drown out any outside noise—Malevolent still heard the piano keys that rang in his ears. He took his time lathering up every inch of his body as if he were waxing his car. *Wax on. Wax off.* Another smile surfaced on his face, pleased with more of the piano tracks. Malevolent wanted to scream to the heavens for this genius work. He didn't want to make the neighbors think that he was crazy. Speaking of this genius—Portia, that is—after this, he was going to head right over to see her. Then his smile turned into a frown; he hadn't seen her in days, and no calls at all.

In the early evening hours, the Fairchild home was quiet; not a soul was in sight, only a neighbor walking her dog. The SRT engine could be heard echoing in the distance as it got closer. Simultaneously, the latest black Acura with beaming headlights parked in the driveway, and then the Dodge Challenger stopped short in front of the home with shiny headlights. Malevolent hopped out of the driver's seat, approaching the driveway as Portia and her parents exited the car. Malevolent and Portia embraced each other without saying any words for a moment. Mr. and Mrs. Fairchild nodded to Malevolent as they entered their home.

"Where were you, baby?" Malevolent asked in a somewhat paranoid tone.

"My grandmother is very sick. She's in Smithtown," Portia played it off.

"Thanks for the piano tracks. They're genius, coming from a genius," Malevolent kissed her on the cheek.

"I want you to come to the studio so you can hear more of my stuff," he added.

"I'd love to," Portia said.

"I've got to get to work.... and I'll call you in the morning," Malevolent kissed her hand, noticing the hospital bracelet on her wrist. He then looked closely, noticing Portia's name.

"You said your grandmother was sick," Malevolent's eyebrows arched while his heart pounded in his chest.

Portia shied away, having been caught in a lie. Malevolent grabbed her chin, allowing her to make eye contact with him. "Were you in the hospital?"

Portia burst into tears, sobbing as she buried her head in Malevolent's chest. He had to find out what was going on.

"Portia, what happened?" he asked.

"I was walking in Manhattan and felt dizzy. And then.....I was stretched out on a midtown concrete," Portia sniffled with a lie. She wiped her tears away. "So, the paramedics came right in time. And I'm alright now," she tittered.

Malevolent glared at her, sensing that she might be telling the truth. He hoped she wasn't hiding anything from him. "And they rushed you to the hospital?"

"Yes, they did. And the doctors did a great job of taking care of me," Portia continued to sniffle.

"What was wrong with you?" Malevolent needed further information.

"I was dehydrated and fell out. I have to remember to drink more water instead of so much caffeine," Portia shrugged.

Malevolent wrapped his arms around Portia, not knowing whether to go to work or even to the recording studio for that matter. His spirit was telling him to stay with her and to call out sick. But she convinced him to go to work and to get down to that recording studio to finish the album. He promised Portia he would return to her in the morning so they could spend more time together. Malevolent pecked her on the cheek, hopped in his muscle car, and sped off.

That night, a slender maintenance man slapped a wet, soaking mop on the tile floor as he cleaned it with headsets. He couldn't hear the elevator music that played from the ceiling speakers of the empty supermarket. Of course, the only people there were the night crew. Malevolent swaggered from aisle to aisle with a price machine in his hand. He didn't communicate with anyone because he had Portia on his mind. He couldn't wait until his shift was over, but he had to wait several hours for that. He glanced at the clock on the wall that read 1:23 a.m. The time dragged, and this was going to be a very long night. Nothing exciting would make the time go faster. Then his cellphone vibrated on his hip as he quickly responded to the call. The caller ID read: Benji. Malevolent answered his manager with a sigh.

"Mal! Beautiful news! 'Machete' is streaming live on Sirius XM radio, and people are loving it!" Benji's voice muffled from the receiver.

"Right now?"

"Yes! Turn on the radio!" Benji proceeded excitedly.

Malevolent placed his price gun on the empty shelf, googled the Sirius radio station, clicked the site, and played the live stream. There it played, "Machete."

"Holy shit! My song hit the airwaves!" Malevolent trotted to the office as he dashed to his desk and grabbed the speaker. He blew into it.

"Everyone, check this out!" He placed his cellphone on the table while "Machete" played and echoed into the microphone.

His first single blasted from the supermarket ceiling speakers. The busy employees heard the hip-hop tune their colleague worked so hard on. The store erupted into cheers and applause for his success. Some even danced to the song.

Early that same morning, the birds chirped throughout the peaceful community of Douglaston while the monstrous engine could be heard in the distance. Red pajama-clad Portia peered from her bedroom window on the second floor of her home. Of course, she knew not to entertain company in her sleepwear. But she didn't care; Malevolent was her boyfriend. What was the difference? They were already intimate. Then the black Jaguar parked in front of the home. Portia's heart dropped and began to beat rapidly in her chest. "What the fuck does Loco want?" She laid in bed, pulling the blankets over herself and shutting her eyes. The doorbell chimed as Portia felt the sound vibrations through her body. The aroma of coffee filled the air, along with waffles, syrup, bacon, and fresh fruit. Loco probably came over to Portia's home to bum a meal. Chances were that Loco was probably dysfunctional. His mother didn't cook, and maybe she didn't know how to cook. His father was most likely a deadbeat or a drunk, or some kind of loser? If that was the case, Loco surely had made something of himself, even though he was an asshole. *Give credit where credit is due*. Then the bell rang again. Again, the sound vibrations traveled through her bones and especially into her ears. She covered her entire head with her pillow, turning on her side. Of course, her mother swung the front door open.

"Good morning, Loco. How are you?" her mother's voice could be heard from downstairs.

"Good morning, Mrs. Fairchild. How are you doing?" Loco's voice greeted from downstairs.

"Come in. Would you like some coffee and breakfast?"

Portia tossed in bed, hearing her mother offer this man that's not even her boyfriend something to eat. *"Why did she let him in? Get him the hell out of the house!"* Portia thought. She punched her pillow because Malevolent was on his way. *"And holy crap, if he comes here and Loco is still here, what will he think of me?"* Portia feared. She had to do something to get him out of the house before Malevolent got there.

"Portia! Portia!" her mother called her from the bottom of the staircase.

"Yes!" she answered as she sat upright in her bed.

"Loco's here!" Mrs. Fairchild hollered.

"Okay!" Portia responded. "What the fuck!" she murmured to herself and sighed. She hopped out of her slumber, threw on her robe, and exited her bedroom.

Seconds later, Loco lounged at the kitchen table, eating a plate of waffles and sausage with a glass of orange juice on the side. Mrs. Fairchild stood over the stove continuing to fix breakfast with a tea kettle on the back burner. Portia rushed into the kitchen, grabbing Loco's plate and scraping his food into the trash.

"What are you doing, Portia? Why are you tossing it out?" Mrs. Fairchild threw her hands in the air.

"Portia, babe!" Loco said.

"You've got to get out of here! Go home or somewhere!" Portia's voice bellowed through the house.

"Your father's sleeping, Portia!" Mrs. Fairchild turned off the tea kettle, which immediately started to whistle on the stove.

"I don't care! Loco, you've got to go!" Portia opened the front door, gesturing for him to leave.

"Thank you for the meal, Mrs. Fairchild. It was a pleasure," Loco played it off.

"Anytime!" Mrs. Fairchild said, waving to him.

"There won't be a next time," Portia slammed the door. She dashed upstairs to her bedroom, closing her door. Portia peered through her sheer curtains at Loco driving away in his Jaguar.

An hour later, the Dodge Challenger parked in front of the Fairchild home with its screeching brakes. The engine shut down and Malevolent exited the driver's seat. He swaggered to the front door and rang the doorbell. Portia immediately opened the door, rushing into her lover's arms. He reciprocated the affection while their embrace was tight around each other's waists. Portia's hug felt akin to an anaconda's deathly squeeze, ready to suck the life out of him. She didn't cry, but Malevolent felt her body trembling.

"Portia, what's wrong?" Malevolent looked her in the eye.

"Nothing," Portia shrugged, still not telling him what was going on.

Malevolent sensed something, and it frightened Portia as she constantly avoided eye contact with him when he asked her a question.

"You're trembling, Portia. What's wrong?" Malevolent asked again as they made their way back into the house.

"Nothing," Portia responded seconds later while they sat on the sofa. Malevolent cradled her in his arms like a baby.

"You keep saying that, Portia," he said again. He kissed her on the forehead.

Portia toughened up, playing it off as usual, and engaged in a passionate kiss with Malevolent. She hoped that her affection would make him stop asking so many questions. Even though she was paranoid, she attempted to alter his attention. She put an immediate smile on her face and asked about his night shift. Malevolent told her that "Machete" played on the radio and that his colleagues at his job heard it. Portia's eyes bulged due to the great news, and that Malevolent had to get down to the studio. To celebrate the news, Portia offered to make him a special breakfast. She kissed him on the lips and sprung from the couch to whip something up in the kitchen for this upcoming star.

An hour later, Malevolent sat at the kitchen table, devouring the last piece of waffle from his plate. He accidentally dropped the fork, which clanked on the plate and startled Portia. Her eyes widened while her hand was on her heart. "Sorry," he apologized, wiping his mouth with his napkin. Malevolent noticed the fear on her face, rubbing her back.

"That's okay," Portia lied again. Malevolent felt something wasn't right with his girlfriend and wanted to get to the bottom of it. He hugged her, hoping he could get whatever it was out of her. Instead, he told her about his plans as Portia rested in his arms and quiet. Malevolent had high hopes for his career, their lives as husband and wife, and little ones. Still, she remained silent, listening to his dreams. Dreams. That's what they were, nothing but hopes and desires for something that might not even occur. Portia didn't understand why she was feeling negatively toward Malevolent. He was so busy working and then heading off to the studio to finish his album. The truth is that maybe Malevolent would find another woman in the industry. Chances were he was probably attracted to Jazzy and some other groupies. There were so many women coming in and out of that studio. Portia witnessed these money-hungry girls hanging around Loco and his friends. She figured maybe she should end their relationship. She didn't want to waste his time so they could both move on. Anyway, Portia needed to focus on her craft and create her own lane. The glistening ring on her finger proceeded to bling, bling, and she didn't want to give it up. It was so pretty, but if things didn't seem promising for them, then she would give it back. Then she thought to wear it for a while and see what would happen between them. Portia then snapped out of her deep thoughts as Malevolent kissed on the cheek.

"Baby, are you alright?"

"Yes, I'm fine," Portia smiled and kissed him back on the cheek.

And as usual, Malevolent stood up from his chair and had to go home to get some sleep because he needed his energy. By Malevolent abruptly dismissing himself, Portia began to have second thoughts. Portia escorted him to the front door as they gave their last kiss. Portia didn't even walk him to his car as she usually did which made the atmosphere between them awkward. Were they growing apart? Or maybe it's because Malevolent had the graveyard shift at his job and had to finish his project. And Portia was just tired. Tired of this unseen drama that occurred. Unseen by Malevolent, who had no awareness of what was going on. Or did he know but didn't bother to utter a word? Yes, Portia was to blame as well. She didn't want to seem like the cause of this tension. It was just best for her to allow their love to gradually fade away. Portia watched from the front door while the Dodge Challenger sped off before she closed it.

CHAPTER EIGHTEEN

A month later, the remarkable lights of Times Square enhanced the city's ambiance, providing tourists with a quintessential New York experience. Theaters, films, restaurants, and additional activities offered increased opportunities for urban recreation. Digital billboards, advertisements, and other business activities facilitated a continuous display. Thousands flocked to the Broadway district, having their photos taken with characters costumed as Spider-Man, Captain America, and others. An immense crowd was captivated by a large digital display of Malevolent performing his song "Machete" in a recording studio. The audience danced to the video of this emerging rapper. Subsequently, Malevolent's collaborative effort with Joe Jose, entitled "I Ain't New to This," was performed. The audience applauded Joe Jose's rap verse, clutching imitation black roses and a flyer advertising the forthcoming album "Mourning Rose." Malevolent's promotion team distributed flyers and artificial black roses to their new fans. From all vantage points, digital billboards showcased the album cover of the black rose accompanied by a retro microphone. Clips of the *"Boom! In the Night"* music video played, creating an eerie feel in the atmosphere, sending chills down the spines of spectators who gasped at the creepy piano piece. Not a single person in the street crowd remained dry-eyed while witnessing the tragic events. A weeping young woman held the black rose as she was embraced by her friends. The fans downloaded "Mourning Rose" to their cellphones from Spotify, Apple iTunes, and other online music vendors. Furthermore, they recorded videos of Malevolent's performance on their cellphones. That was, in essence, their inaugural complimentary concert.

MC MALEVOLENT featuring DJ LOCO
"MOURNING ROSE"

1. "Machete"
2. "Boom! In the Night"
3. "Roses are Black"
4. "Boom-Bap Clap"
5. "Repping Queens"
6. "I Ain't New to This" featuring Joey Jose
7. "Shitload"
8. "Tracking My Steps"

On the scene were hip-hop reporters asking fans questions about this upcoming rapper and looking forward to seeing him live. CNN, a major news outlet, had their music reporter right in the midst of it all, giving almost every person in the crowd a chance to express themselves.

"Are you excited about the 'Mourning Rose album?" the CNN music reporter asked, pointing the microphone at a young guy.

"Yes! Hell yes! Look at this gorgeous cover!" the young guy held up the "Mourning Rose" rack card.

"That is a gorgeous cover! What's your favorite track on the album?" the CNN music reporter's voice echoed through the microphone before placing it back in front of the fan's mouth.

"Roses are Black," the fan responded, lowering his voice.

"What does that track mean to you?" the CNN reporter asked.

"Because I lost someone very close to me. You and everyone can relate to this track," the young guy added, placing his hand over his heart.

"That's right. I definitely agree," the CNN reporter returned the microphone to the fan.

Lounging in a chair in the living room, Portia watched the news of her lover's success on her flat-panel television, along with her parents. Portia heard the piano tracks she created for Malevolent echoing throughout Times Square. She was proud that she created something so beautiful and exciting. Portia hoped she would get credit for it and some exposure. In most cases, people behind the scenes—whether it be in movies, music, art, or a product or business—really don't get any credit for their talents. Mr. Fairchild gave his daughter the thumbs-up while smiling at the piano playing coming directly from the television into their living room.

"I wish they would interview you, Portia," Mrs. Fairchild leaned forward toward the television from the sofa.

"It's not about me, Mom. This is Alejandro's success," Portia shrugged her shoulders.

"This is the way things work in the world: the talentless get all of the credit," Mr. Fairchild indirectly insulted.

“Are you serious right now?” Portia’s eyes widened at her father’s disrespect. “Alejandro is very talented!”

“Well, I’m sorry. I can’t get into all of this rap crap,” her father insulted again. “Portia, focus on classical music and jazz, for Christ’s sake! Malevolent—Alejandro, for that matter—is full of dreams, and he’ll be just another no-name rapper in a few years. That music industry is no good. And who the hell is that Loco clown? He looks like something’s wrong with him. I’m grateful that he helped you when you passed out, but I don’t want you with him either!” her father continued to ramble.

“What makes you think I would get with Loco if I’m with Malevolent?” Portia wondered.

“I don’t know. Maybe because of his heroism. I guess,” Mr. Fairchild waved his hands in the air.

Then the doorbell chimed as Portia sprang from her chair to see who was at the door. Her father proceeded to argue with her from the living room. She ignored him, wishing he would shut up. Portia swung the door open, noticing a delivery man holding a large bouquet of roses.

“Portia Fairchild?” the delivery man smiled, holding a computerized tablet in his hands.

“Yes, that’s me,” she opened the glass screen door as the delivery man handed her the roses. “Sign here,” the delivery man added. Portia signed the receipt.

“Thank you,” said the delivery man as he headed back toward his truck. Portia stood there, holding the beautiful roses in her hands. There was also a card. She slammed the front door and headed toward the living room. Her mother noticed the floral bouquet, and her eyes bulged.

“Those are beautiful, Portia! Who are they from?”

Portia placed the flowers on the coffee table and read the card. Mrs. Fairchild rose from the sofa and sniffed the roses as a smile surfaced on her face. On the contrary, Portia's face wasn't pleased with what the card read. She ripped the card in half and knocked the flowers to the floor. Luckily, the vase wasn't glass, and only some water and dirt splattered on the floor. Portia dashed upstairs to her bedroom and slammed the door, shaking the house.

"Portia! Why did you do that?" Mrs. Fairchild cleaned up the floral mess. "Honey, could you help me here?"

"Portia, what's the problem?" her father hollered, even though she was already in her bedroom. "I'll get the broom. Don't touch the dirt," Mr. Fairchild marched to the kitchen for a broom.

Portia's mother noticed the half-ripped note on the floor. She picked it up, it read.

Hey Portia,

Thanks to you, Malevolent is going to have a successful album. I want to take you to dinner to discuss further projects and us!!!

Talk to you soon,

Loco

Meanwhile, Portia paced her bedroom floor with her cellphone to her ear. Her face trembled, hoping Malevolent answered. It rang once. Then a second time. A third time, and then a fourth, and it went directly to voicemail. Portia sat on the edge of her bed, rocking.

"Yo, this is Malevolent. Leave your name and number and I'll holla back at you. Peace. Beep!" the voicemail delivered.

"Malevolent, it's me, Portia. Congrats on your album's release. I wish I was there to enjoy the celebration, but I'm not feeling up to it. Still, please contact me because we have to talk. I love you. Bye," Portia ended her call. She tossed her cellphone on the bed, curled up in a fetal position, and closed her eyes. She would love for her and Malevolent to travel to another place where no harm would come to them. They would have all the money in the world to live comfortably and continue with their aspirations. But Portia had to face the ugly reality: Loco was pursuing her hard, and Malevolent probably didn't have the slightest idea about what was going on.

CHAPTER NINETEEN

Handsome, pudgy-faced, legendary hip-hop radio host icon DJ Kirk blew into the pop-filtered microphone, wearing headsets while lounging on a burgundy curvy sofa. Directly behind the cushioned couch was a backdrop of the Manhattan night skyline along a brick wall with photos of rappers and celebrities from the past to the present. "Welcome to the DJ Kirk show! I would like to introduce my next guests. These guys are brilliant. With no further ado, straight out of Queens! Let's give it up to MC Malevolent and DJ Loco in the building!" DJ Kirk applauded along with his colleagues who had been affiliated with him from the start of his career. Malevolent relaxed on the right side of the comfy sofa while the microphone was a little too far from his mouth, which would cause listeners not to hear him. He knew he had to sit upright and tell the world his story. As for Loco, he hunched over his microphone, waiting to give the world a taste of what he was about. Both men didn't make eye contact with one another while DJ Kirk asked questions, sitting in the center of the sofa.

"Thank you for having me, Kirk!" Malevolent paid his respects and saluted him.

"What up, Kirk! Much respect!" Loco gave him the thumbs up.

Malevolent's heart throbbed fast in his chest because this was his first interview that could make or break him. He had to make sure he said the right things that would interest listeners. All he had to do was play it cool. He was the frontman, so he had nothing to worry about.

"Congrats on your new album, 'Mourning Rose,'" DJ Kirk's voice muffled in his microphone.

"Thank you, Kirk," Malevolent smiled and nodded. He noticed how Loco reacted to the question, as he didn't show any enthusiasm. Loco slightly smiled and focused his eyes in the opposite direction like a jealous child. Malevolent couldn't understand why Loco was acting like this. He had a huge hand in this project and would get more money from Malevolent's labor.

"Before I get to my first question, I just want to show the audience this gorgeous cover. This black rose is breathtaking!" DJ Kirk held up a large flyer of the album cover.

"Thank you!" Malevolent said, as he noticed Loco continuing to focus his eyes in the opposite direction.

"How did you come up with the idea? Was this a collaboration or one person's idea?" DJ Kirk asked while glancing between this hip-hop duo. He acknowledged Loco's contributions to the project. Loco didn't react to the question as he continued to shift his eyes in the other direction. He drifted into another world, with nothing on his mind for the moment. Malevolent noticed his best friend's odd behavior. He hoped this interview would go smoothly. No bumps. No cracks. No tension. Even though there was hostility between the longtime friends, Loco smiled and played along.

"A black rose isn't a real rose, but it can be created. And it represents death and anything dark, hostile, and all that negative shit. My father took his life when I was seven," Malevolent placed his hand on his heart.

"Oh! I'm sorry for your loss, man!" DJ Kirk gave his condolences. Malevolent proceeded to explain his life and noticing Loco looking at the floor. He wanted to scream into the microphone to get his best friend's attention, but that would only make him look bad. So, he continued to tell his story.

Malevolent's eyes welled with tears as he explained that his relationship with his mother was strained, and he held her somewhat accountable for the events that had transpired. He shut his eyes to suppress the tears. He preferred to avoid displaying any vulnerability to his new audience. Enabling fans to hear his emotions was a positive measure, demonstrating his human qualities— not a figure of celebrity status who is immune to adversity.

DJ Kirk requested one of his colleagues to provide tissues and bottled water to comfort his guest. A young woman retrieved the water and tissue. Loco of course, didn't offer comfort as he had previously done, given his current self-centeredness. Again, his gaze remained averted and he wished that Malevolent would find closure regarding his father's demise. *"We're all going to die someday, so get the fuck over it!"*

Malevolent received water and tissues from DJ Kirk's female colleague, who rushed toward him. "Thanks," he sniffled and wiped his tears with the Kleenex.

"Would you like to continue with your story, Malevolent? Or do you wish to stop?" DJ Kirk asked.

"We can stop! The only thing is that the album is telling of my history," Malevolent said, poking his chest out. Loco then focused his eyes back on his best friend and was happy to hear that Malevolent wasn't going to cry, embarrassing himself and Loco.

"DJ Loco! My man, you've been around a long time. You have a history in the music business for about twelve years," DJ Kirk saluted him.

"Yes, it's been a long time, struggling to get the right artists. I produced some one-hit wonders, but I wanted to have an artist that wanted a career in hip-hop. Malevolent and I were best friends since high school, and his lyrics were tight. I told him when he was ready to flow, let me know, and we could go. And here we are," Loco made eye contact with Malevolent, nodding.

"Yes, we are," Malevolent responded.

"I noticed on some of your tracks, such as 'Boom! In the Night!' It has an eerie piano track on it," DJ Kirk complimented.

"Yeah, that's my girl Portia. She's...," Malevolent was rudely interrupted.

"...a classical pianist. Portia's a genius. This young lady could play at Carnegie Hall. And one day she will. And she's beautiful. You need to see her, Kirk. You'll be like, 'Damn, she's fine,'" Loco continued to tell DJ Kirk about Malevolent's girlfriend. Malevolent glared at Loco for rudely cutting him off. Loco didn't stop talking about this special lady who had captured Loco's heart.

"I discovered her talents. Portia can play anything on the piano...," Loco said, before being interrupted.

"...and I first discovered Portia as she and I exchanged conversations over lunch while she told me about her musical dreams and her family," Malevolent returned the rudeness back to Loco. While Malevolent spoke fondly about Portia, Loco became fiery red in the face and blew into the microphone.

"Where did you guys have lunch?"

"What?" Malevolent sat upright, his face turning red.

"Where did you take Portia?" Loco shrugged.

"What does it matter?" Malevolent gritted his teeth.

"It does matter. A special girl like Portia should be showered with the best," Loco added.

Malevolent couldn't believe what he was hearing. Did Loco have a thing for Portia? He and DJ Kirk glanced at one another and even the radio staff that was present during the interview.

"If Portia was mine, I would definitely wine and dine her," Loco grinned.

"Why the fuck are you speaking about my lady? We're supposed to be discussing my album. Did you forget?"

"Our album."

"True. Let's stay focused," Malevolent argued.

"Yo, Kirk! You need to come down to the studio to hear Portia play?" Loco got off the subject of their album.

DJ Kirk raised an eyebrow, giving Loco the side-eye. He wondered if he was drunk or something because he should be talking about their music here. He also wondered what the listeners were thinking. What was going through their minds about this rap duo?

"Get my girl's name out of your mouth! And stay focused, motherfucker!" Malevolent got out of character.

"So what! You've got a fine-ass woman. I'm just complimenting your tastes!" Loco hollered into the microphone.

"It sounds like you want a taste of her!" Malevolent rocked in his seat.

"And what if I do? Then what the fuck!" Loco threw his hands in the air.

"What the fuck! What the fuck do you mean, what the fuck!" Malevolent stood up from his side of the sofa as Loco did the same. They were about to get up in each other's faces as

Benji, DJ Kirk, and the radio staff got between the two men, ready to break it up.

"Yo! Malevolent and Loco, what the fuck are you doing?" Benji got between them, pushing them away from each other. DJ Kirk realized the commotion could be heard by his listeners. "Cut the interview short! Cut it! Cut it!" he alerted his staff members. The staff members disconnected the plugs as the interview was ceased. Malevolent and Loco's voices echoed into the lobby of the building as security intervened.

"Stop being so touchy and shit!" Loco taunted him.

"Don't think about getting touchy!" Malevolent and Benji walked away from Loco. Benji placed his hand on Malevolent's shoulder, escorting him to the elevators on the other side, along with two security guards.

"I just might get touchy with Portia! You better keep her close!" Loco's voice echoed in the distance.

"Ignore him, Malevolent! Please, man!" Benji pushed Malevolent toward the elevators. "Don't think about confronting him!"

Benji, Malevolent, and the security guards approached the elevators. Malevolent pounded his fist on the brick wall continuously. "Some fucking shit! History repeating itself!"

Benji continuously pressed the elevator button to go down. Then slowly the steel doors opened as Malevolent and Benji dashed inside. The doors closed.

While the elevator descended to the ground floor seconds later, Malevolent paced the steel box before his manager. He and Benji didn't exchange any words, only the elevator music played. Benji focused his eyes at the bright lights ceiling elevator, tapping his foot.

"What the fuck has gotten into you guys?" Benji shook his head.

"I have no idea what the fuck is going on with Loco," Malevolent shrugged, leaning in the corner.

"So, that's why you guys were acting oddly in the restaurant?" Benji glaring him right in the eye.

"I don't know, Benji," Malevolent threw his arms up.

"You should know, Malevolent!" Benji turned away, shaking his head.

"What?" Malevolent asked.

"What do you mean, 'what'? You're opening for Joey Jose at Madison Square Garden, and then you've got your album release party! You guys are going to have to squash this shit!" Benji pointed him like a child.

"I know!" Malevolent stomped his foot.

"You better know!" Benji hollered at him. Then the elevator door opened as they swaggered into the first-floor lobby, exiting the building.

The next morning, instrumental rap tracks played in Loco's black Jaguar as he sped down Junction Boulevard, not caring about motorists, pedestrians, or the cops. He feared no one because he was so enraged with Malevolent during their interview. A whirlwind of crazy thoughts went through his mind. Loco envisioned taking a nine-millimeter handgun and blowing Malevolent's head off, or have his entourage beat Malevolent until he drowned in a pool of his own blood. Loco didn't want to risk going to the slammer; he'd have to come up with another plan. But for now, he drove around his neighborhood of Rego Park, halting his vehicle at a red traffic light. His Jaguar screeched to a stop as Boogey swaggered across the street. Loco's eyes widened, honking the horn of his car.

"Boogey!" Loco rolled down his window. Boogey's face lit up while holding two bags of groceries in his hands. He hopped into the passenger seat, closing the door. Loco proceeded to drive around his neighborhood.

"What's up, Loco? I just came from the supermarket for your mother!" Boogey placed the groceries in the backseat.

"Thanks for looking out!" Loco bumped fists with Boogey. He gave his neighborhood friend a hundred-dollar bill. "Here you go, man."

"Thanks, man," Boogey took the cash and then nodded to the pulsing rhythmic sound. Then another instrumental music track played. Boogey glanced at Loco who focused on his driving and didn't utter a word. Boogey sensed his friend was in another world. "When are you going to put me on, Loco?"

"Put you on to what?" Loco sneered from the corner of his eye.

"When are you going to let me get in the booth?" Boogey sighed.

"When you come up with some cash and then we'll do something," Loco replied in a stern tone.

"After you and Mal get on then it will be my turn, right?"

"Right! When you come up with that cash! Right?' Loco made eye contact with him.

"Right!" Boogey cackled.

"And aren't you supposed to be looking for a job or something to come up with the cash for your musical endeavors?" Loco shrugged.

"You're right," Boogey continued to snickered.

"How is she doing?" Loco asked about his mother while focusing his eyes on the road.

"She's good! Go see her!" Boogey advised.

"Got you!" Loco nodded.

Down a long corridor of an apartment building, Loco swaggered with the two grocery bags in his hand. His relationship with his mother, Ines Porter, raised him alone due to his father running in and out of their lives with broken promises. Loco's father was a womanizer; he chased women and flirted with them right before his mother's eyes. He didn't care how much he hurt Ines. His infidelities went on for years, even creating outside children. Finally, he left them for good because not only did his father hurt his mother, but Mr. Porter also did a number on Loco. Loco always wondered how many siblings he might have in the world. They would probably come out of the woodwork when he became a famous DJ. He stopped before an apartment door and heard a game show playing from a television. He knocked on the door, knowing that he should've had a key to enter. He should've made a copy of the key, but he gave it to his mother because he moved on with his life. Then an ebony, long-haired, thirty-something Latina swung the door open, smiling, dressed in scrubs.

"Hola, Lorenzo!" the home aide greeted.

"What up, Lita?" Loco swaggered into the apartment as the door closed.

Lounging in a cushioned recliner, Mrs. Porter cackled at the game show as saliva streamed from the corner of her mouth. She wiped it with a napkin from her half-paralyzed face.

"Who is it, Lita?" she stuttered.

"It's me, Mom!" Loco stepped into the living room, making his presence known. He placed a kiss on her cheek. He glared at her for a second and wanted to cry because of his mother's suffering. Loco eyed his mother's half paralyzed body which was from head to toe.

"I missed you. How's my baby?" Mrs. Porter slurred her words.

"I'm cool," Loco responded. He had to get out of there

because he couldn't stand seeing his mother in her condition. He believed his father was the cause of her stroke. But he couldn't help but stay with her for a while until she fell asleep. So, he did just that.

An hour later, a pot of chicken soup bubbled on the stove over a low flame, along with a teapot on the burner behind it. Lita stirred the soup in the pot and turned off the teapot as it started to whistle. Loco sat in the chair, noticing Lita's body in her tight scrubs. Her plump buttocks and camel-toed vagina caused a rush of blood to his penis, getting it hard and ready for action. Loco peeked into the living room, where his mother was fast asleep.

Moaning, groaning, nudity, and thrusting occurred in Loco's childhood bedroom while Lita lay on her back with her legs wrapped around his waist. The bed creaked due to hard pumping and Loco's two-hundred-pound body on top of Lita's. He always wanted to hit it, not necessarily quit it because Lita cared for his sick mother.

"Lita!" Mrs. Porter cried from the living room.

"Yes, Mrs. Porter!" Lita yelled.

"Where are you?" Mrs. Porter cried.

Lita and Loco sprang from the bed and got dressed quickly, and fled from the bedroom.

Moments later, Mrs. Porter fed herself with a spoon as best she could with the help of her home aide. Loco lounged on the sofa, noticing how his mother was doing, and Lita was the best nurse for his mother. He glanced at his wristwatch, stood to his feet, and kissed his mother on the cheek.

"I've got to go," Loco said.

"When are you coming back?" his mother slurred.

"I don't know," Loco shrugged.

"How's Alejandro?" his mother asked.

"He's alright, I guess," Loco responded. He kissed her again.

"I'll walk you to the door," Lita strutted to the front door, opening it. Loco gave her a one-hundred-dollar bill, kissing her on the cheek and exiting the apartment.

Soothing R&B music echoed through another well-lit hallway of a Queens apartment building in the same town, not too far from where Loco's mother resided. He swaggered to the last blue door in the corner, balling his fist and preparing to knock on the door. He remembered how he treated Jazzy and he didn't care about her. He figured he'd give her a good talking to, or a good fuck would do the trick. But he already got some; but there's always round two. He pounded on the apartment door as if he were her husband. The music was loud, so of course, there was no answer. Loco pounded and pounded until Jazzy swung the door open. "What the hell is your problem! Banging on my door like that! What do you want?"

"Turn the music down! You're disturbing the peace!" Loco attempted to force his way into her place. Jazzy blocked his path.

"No!"

"Let me in; we have to talk!" Loco pushed Jazzy out of the way and made his way into her apartment. She then slammed the door.

Minutes later, Loco turned off Jazzy's computer that was playing loud music. He then made himself right at home, placing his feet on her chair. Jazzy marched over to him and pushed his feet off her furniture.

"Get your dirty boots off my chair! Are you crazy?"

"Sorry," Loco apologized kindly.

"What do you want?"

"I need a favor."

"What is it this time? Do you want something to eat because I'm cooking pasta right now? Or is it some booty? You want some booty?"

"No. No."

"Yes, you do."

"I'm inviting you to our album release party; bring your girlfriends."

"Why?"

"Because."

"Because what, Loco?" Jazzy folded her arms.

"Portia has a nice ring," he added.

"And what does that have to do with me?" Jazzy asked.

"I want you to get it."

"What! And then what?"

"Give it to me," Loco answered.

"And then?" Jazzy's eyebrows arched.

Loco reached into his pocket, standing up from the couch, and gave her some cash. "And here you go."

Jazzy counted the money, shaking her head, then threw it in Loco's face. "Are you treating me like some kind of trick?"

"Yes, you are. You're a trick. A 3-0-4. A thot and all of the above," Loco turned fiery red in the face.

Seconds later, screams, thuds, rumbling, and crashing of furniture and glass erupted from the apartment where hell has erupted. Jazzy's pleaded for Loco to stop with his rage. He smacked her around constantly, releasing his wrath. He cursed up a storm while his irate tone could be heard for miles. The terror echoed throughout the building.

CHAPTER TWENTY

Traditional Japanese music—Hogaku—played from the ceiling speakers of a Japanese restaurant in Forest Hills, Queens. Everything, from wall décor to furniture to the floor, reflected the ambience of this rich culture. Seated at a table for two in the corner, Malevolent and Portia held menus in their hands with silence between them. Malevolent glanced between his menu and then at Portia. He also looked over his shoulder as if something or someone disturbed him. Portia did the same, peering from behind her menu and then back at him. She wanted to tell him about the incident with Loco, but he would find out later. Yes, she had heard the radio interview, which was an absolute disaster. Now, everyone knew her name, and she had some fame in the hip-hop game.

Malevolent slammed his menu down on the table, staring at Portia as if she was at fault for the situation surrounding the hip-hop duo. "Tell me something, Portia. Are you attracted to Loco in any way?" he leaned forward in his chair.

"No!" Portia raised her voice, attracting the attention of restaurant guests.

"Keep your voice down!" Malevolent grinded his teeth. He glanced over his shoulders at the other diners.

"No," she whispered. "Why would you think that?"

"I know you heard the radio interview," Malevolent said.

"Yes, I heard it. I listened to it to support you," Portia sighed.

"The entire interview was about you. You've got a name now, Portia," Malevolent leaned back in his chair, glaring at her with disgust.

"I don't appreciate the way you're looking at me! You're acting as if I did something wrong!" Portia slammed her menu on the table and stormed away. For a moment, Malevolent remained in his seat, not bothering to go after her. He didn't glance over his shoulder to see what direction she went in. The only direction he knew was Portia exiting the establishment. He looked around at the restaurant guests, who didn't pay him any mind. He figured he might as well dine alone. This was an unusual setting for a rapper: no woman, no friend, no family, and not even business colleagues. Malevolent fidgeted in his chair, glancing over his shoulder to see if anyone noticed.

Then a slender Japanese server approached his table, bowing. "Is everything okay?"

"Yes. I'm cool. Hold my table. I'll be right back!" Malevolent stormed out of the restaurant.

Meanwhile, Portia stormed down the street, maneuvering between pedestrians without looking back. She took long strides, trying to get to the train station and go home. Maybe her father was right about her dating a rapper. They were nothing but trouble. These artists would either go to jail, have baby mama drama, get shot, or killed. Portia needed to focus on her own music; she had talent. She didn't want credit for her piano tracks on his album. She just wanted to be out of this mess while setting her sights on the station up ahead. As she kept up her pace, a sharp migraine jabbed at her temple, like someone poking her with a needle.

Suddenly, someone was right on her trail and grabbed her arm. "Where are you going?" Malevolent pulled her close, wrapping his arms around her tightly. Portia fought to wrestle free, not wanting to cause a scene like the one in the city. But she quickly stopped resisting; this was the man she loved, and she hoped he loved her back. Portia hoped that her body wouldn't collapse onto the pavement either. Malevolent eyed her as he escorted her down the block. No words were exchanged, but their eyes spoke volumes. She could sense that Malevolent had something on his mind.

"Why doesn't Loco tell him?" Portia thought. But then, Loco might twist the truth, making it seem like he wasn't pursuing her.

Within seconds, Portia and Malevolent marched back into the Japanese restaurant and took their seats at the table they had occupied earlier. The waiter dashed over, bowing and holding a computerized tablet in his hand. "May I take your order, sir? Are you ready?"

"Yes," Malevolent nodded and looked over his menu quickly. He signaled to Portia to order something to eat.

"I'll have the steak and shrimp with white rice," Portia ordered, glaring at Malevolent in return.

"And I'll have the same," Malevolent smiled, handing the menus back to the server.

"And to drink?"

"Water!" Portia answered tersely. Malevolent reached under the table and pinched her.

"Ouch! What's your problem?" Portia smacked his hand.

"Keep your voice down!" Malevolent grinded his teeth. "We'll have two cokes," he said, smiling at the server.

"Okay, thank you," the Japanese server said as he walked away.

"Don't leave like that again! Why are you embarrassing me?" Malevolent glanced over his shoulders.

"You're embarrassing yourself, Mal," Portia folded her arms, leaning back in her chair.

"Are you serious?" Malevolent asked.

"Am I embarrassing you because you're a hot rapper and everyone knows your name?" Portia taunted him.

"Stop! Now, Portia," Malevolent pounded his fist on the table, grinding his teeth. They both looked around to see if any guests noticed the tension between them. From across the dining area, a group of five guests was seated at a long table, glaring and pointing at Portia and Malevolent.

One of the young ladies approached Malevolent's table with a pen and a flyer for the "Mourning Rose" album. "Hello, MC Malevolent," the pretty young woman said shyly, playing with her hair.

"Yes, that's me. How are you doing?" Malevolent shook her hand.

"I knew it was you. My friends and I love your music," the young lady beckoned her friends, who rushed over to the budding star. Three young women in their early twenties and a young man of the same age joined them. The guy bumped fists with Malevolent while the girls huddled around with their cellphones, snapping photos. Portia sat there with her arms folded but had a pleasant smile on her face. His fans recognized him, and soon he would have them nationwide and internationally. Portia knew this was something she would have to deal with.

During the drive home, Portia slept in the passenger seat of Malevolent's muscle car. He constantly glanced at her before focusing back on the road. He didn't disturb her; she was probably tired, tired of his antics, tired of the music business, and tired of the entire bullshit surrounding it all. He wondered if she would attend his album release party. He wanted Portia there to support him, and he loved her deeply. He couldn't deal with her absence; if she wasn't there, the groupies would be ready to gobble him up like ravenous tigers.

Malevolent didn't mean to sound like a possessive boyfriend, but he wanted his love with him to celebrate his success. The only person he had to keep an eye on was Loco. He had a very sneaky side; Loco would stab anyone in the back. He was cutthroat, in a cutthroat business, and would cut anyone's throat to get what he wanted. He would probably do his own mother in. Malevolent had a gut feeling that he would try to push up on Portia. And even had a gut instinct that Portia would eventually fall into the arms of another man. Just like his mother fell into another man's arms, leading to his father taking his life. Malevolent would ensure he wouldn't go out that way. No disrespect to his deceased father, but it was what it was. Malevolent respected a man who fought for what he wanted and who he loved. Men fight. They fight for power, for resources, money, and women. If he ever had to throw fists for Portia, then so be it.

In a matter of minutes, the Dodge Challenger pulled up to the curb before the Fairchild residence, its headlights beaming. The monstrous engine rumbled as Malevolent turned it off. All he heard was crickets chirping as he stared at Portia, snoozing like a baby. He stroked her hair and rubbed her cheek, not wanting to wake her. Maybe he could take her to work with him; it was his last day, so what was the difference? He then kissed her on the cheek and forehead.

Portia slowly opened her eyes, noticing her lover occupying the driver's seat. She grasped his hand with a slight smile, and for some strange reason, closed her eyes again. Maybe Portia didn't realize she was home, or perhaps she thought she was dreaming and felt she was in her own bed.

"Portia, baby," Malevolent whispered in her ear. Again, she opened her eyes, sitting upright in the passenger seat and looking around.

"Wow, I'm home. I thought I was dreaming," Portia shook her head, realizing she was back to reality.

"Baby, I've got to get to work."

"It's your last day," Portia stroked his cheek.

"And then I'll be well on my way, hopefully to a successful life," Malevolent shrugged.

"You will," Portia laid a passionate kiss on Malevolent's lips.

"We will," he replied in return.

Just then, the porch light turned on, and Mrs. Fairchild stood in the doorway.

"I've got to go. Good night," Malevolent said, giving Portia one last kiss.

"Good night," she replied. Portia exited the passenger seat of the SRT-8 vehicle, slamming the door. She trotted up the steps and into the house, waving and blowing a kiss to Malevolent. He smiled and started up his engine, speeding off.

Later that night, a worker's computerized time clock read 10:57 p.m. as Malevolent punched in his ID number as the machine beeped. His mind was focused on getting the establishment ready for the next morning. He swaggered into the main office, where Natasha lounged in a recliner in front of the computer. She stroked the keys, finishing up her last tasks before ending her shift. He greeted her and grabbed the price gun from the charger. Nothing felt out of the ordinary; it was business as usual. The computerized price gun's beeping drove him crazy, but he wouldn't have to listen to that sound anymore. Soon, he'd hear cheers from fans, the clanking of wine glasses, the "Cha-Ching" of money, and the "Ding, Ding, da-ding" of wedding bells.

Malevolent strode through the produce department, noticing only one stock boy loading a few veggies and fruits on the shelves. He didn't think anything of it; he figured the rest were in the break room or hadn't come in yet. As he made his way into the bakery department, he noticed it was empty. "Where the fuck is everyone?" he muttered. Proceeding to the seafood department, he saw only one employee and waved. He marched down the first aisle, approaching another computerized time clock and noticed the time. It was a minute to eleven p.m. and his heart raced in his chest. "Holy shit!"

"Attention all shoppers! Just Right is now closed. Please bring your last purchases to the checkout, and thank you for shopping at Just Right! Good night!" Natasha announced over the loudspeaker.

Malevolent took a deep breath as his coworker made the announcement. "Thanks, Natasha!" he shouted throughout the store, hoping she heard him. He made his way up and down each aisle, noticing more new faces as he greeted them with waves and smiles. He noticed a shopping cart of returns and attempted to ask the front end who it belonged to. It was filled with crushed cookies, cereal boxes, dented canned goods, and expired items. He wheeled it to the backroom, where the sound of the baler drowned out the noise in the air. "Hey, get rid of this stuff! It's damages!" Malevolent shouted, handing the cart to a maintenance worker. He continued striding through the heavy swing doors and finished checking the rest of the aisles until he reached the frozen section. He eyed the breakfast entrees and side dishes—French fries, onion rings, breads, fruits, veggies, and more.

"Alejandro! Alejandro! Come to the backroom!" Natasha announced over the loudspeaker again.

"What?!" he murmured to himself but didn't head to the backroom. Instead, he continued checking every aisle. He marched into the dairy department, eyeing the sour creams, cottage cheeses, cheese, eggs, milk, and other items. He noticed a yogurt was stocked in the wrong place and scanned it with the price to see where it went. It beeped.

"That fuckin' sound," he mumbled, placing it in its rightful spot.

"Alejandro, come to the backroom!" Natasha announced again.

"Wait!" Malevolent shouted throughout the store. "I'm coming! Damn!"

Minutes later, several employees lounged in the break room, a female employee bit into an apple while flipping through a magazine, a male employee slept in a chair, and another maintenance worker swept the floor. Malevolent marched through the break room, making his way to the backroom. He noticed it was dark as he slid the wooden door open, and the lights came on.

"Surprise!" his colleagues shouted, about twenty-five of them crowding the small room. Black and silver balloons, an enormous photo of Malevolent from one of his photo shoots plastered on the wall, matching tablecloths, paper plates, cups, and plastic utensils decorated the room. A stack of gifts stood in the corner, wrapped in beautiful black and silver paper with cards for his farewell. He received hugs, kisses, pats on the back, and fist bumps, all wishing him the best on his road to success.

CHAPTER TWENTY-ONE

Steel elevator doors opened to an enormous rooftop venue as the intro to “Machete” bellowed throughout the atmosphere. Malevolent swaggered into a crowd of cheering fans, greeting him with fist bumps, handshakes, and pretty women showering him with hugs and kisses. Dozens of artificial black roses adorned the atmosphere, along with warm party lights, black and silver balloons, black ostrich feather centerpieces on tables, and a huge, gorgeous black ostrich feathered centerpiece that looked like a palm tree. This fabulous hip-hop fiesta overlooked the entire New York City landscape, making it a once-in-a-lifetime experience.

Malevolent went straight from his farewell party at his day job to an even bigger celebration for his album’s release. He rushed to the stage where fans stood before him with love and admiration. He performed “Machete” as Loco worked his magic on the turntables.

"I'm Malevolent

Heard that they ain't ready yet
Leave the scene a fuckin' mess
Aiming at your fuckin' head
These bars like a knife
Like a stick like machete
I aim it at your head
Heard nobody ain't ready
Ready
See I'm Malevolent
These rappers up against
Somebody they ain't never seen
Like in the fuckin' flesh,
I leave the scene a mess
Y'all rapping' wit the best
Each time I battle rap like 8 mile
Straight for your heads
These bars they love the blood
Machete wit the cuts
The lava wit the flow
Some vodka on the rocks
The bar's hitting got a bite
Make your stomach drop, drop, drop, drop
I'm Malevolent
Heard that they ain't ready yet
Leave the scene a fuckin' mess
Aiming at your fucking head
These bars like a knife
Like a stick like machete
I aim it at your head
Heard nobody ain't ready
Ready,"

Malevolent continued with his performance moving the crowd. Online hip-hop radio stations, news media, social media influencers, and other promoters were in attendance for this special event. Malevolent loved how so many new fans had come out to support him. Pretty, starstruck young women wore short dresses, skirts, low-cut blouses, tight-fitting pants, and revealing attire to catch the eye of this rising rap artist.

During his performance, he noticed the groupies in the first two rows hoping to get a piece of him by the end of the night. He hoped Portia would show up; then he'd feel better. He was aware he had to cater to his female fan base, but Portia was the one for him. Hopefully, she would understand that. Right now, Malevolent had to focus on the crowd. Loco scratched on the turntables as Malevolent nodded his head to the music, continuing with his show. He didn't think about their beef. He hoped the event would go smoothly because he had worked hard and wanted to avoid any difficulties that might arise. Benji cheered Malevolent and Loco from the side stage, along with colleagues and a couple of reporters. As Loco worked the turntables, he didn't care if Malevolent asked about him about Portia. He was going to be honest and fuck up Malevolent's entire evening. He was crazy like that. Loco's colleagues, friends, and family wondered, "Why would he risk his success on something so stupid?" With all his achievements, he could have anything in the world. He held the world in the palm of his hand. Loco understood their point of view, but he saw it differently. With his resilient mentality, he could screw something up and bounce back in no time at all. If he and Malevolent could go their separate ways business-wise, he wouldn't have a problem finding other hip-hop artists. On top of that, he had the talent for creating "Boom-Bap" sounds and connections to established rappers in the business. But Benji had already booked Loco and Malevolent to open for Joey Jose at Madison Square Garden.

Back to reality, the stage darkened, and a bluish light shone upon Malevolent. He held his head down, praying to God for his success. During his private moment with God, the crowd cheered. Malevolent hoped that God would bless him and protect him from any obstacles and barriers that might come his way. Of course, these challenges came in this chaotic music industry. Nothing in this business was glitzy or glam. Malevolent rapped the song "Roses Are Black"

"Roses are Black,
mourners are blue,
I wished I would've wrestled that pistol from you,
Tears shed,
ashes to ashes,
dust to dust,
How can I trust,
When you went away,
How could I have convinced you to stay,
Roses are black,
mourners are blue,
I wish I would've wrestled that pistol from you,
Roses are black,
mourners are blue,
I wish I would've wrestled that pistol from you
Just a kid not knowing what I did,
I was good in school, not trying to be cool,
no fights,
no talking back, cause I would've got my fuckin'
face smacked,
my mother attacked your spirit,

your character,
and your heart,
Her torture tore you fuckin' apart,
then you met your demise,
tears shed,
ashes to ashes,
dust to dust,
how do I trust,
when you went away,
how could I have convinced you to stay,
Roses are black,
mourners are blue,
I wished I would've wrestled that pistol from you,
Roses are black,
mourners are blue,
I wished I would've wrestled that pistol from you,
Pops rest in peace,
love you,"

looking out into the audience, Malevolent could see no one. He knew that was the point. He was alone, reminiscing about his father's death. He wanted to storm off the stage and call it quits, but he couldn't because this was his work, and he wanted the world to hear his story. He took a glimpse behind him and couldn't see Loco. Maybe it was best he didn't see Loco so he could focus on his performance. After this, maybe he'd go home and drink himself into oblivion. He heard his father's voice echoing in his head as he concluded the song. "To my father, Edgar Valasquez. I love you, Pop!" Malevolent kissed his fingers and held them in the air as a symbol of his undying love for his beloved father. The song touched the hearts of his fans in the audience. There wasn't a dry eye in the crowd; they felt this rapper's pain and had experienced the loss of a loved one. Then fans tossed artificial black roses onto the stage at Malevolent's feet. He noticed the murky flowers, stepping back and feeling grateful to his audience. He thanked them and looked forward to a meet-and-greet, taking photographs and signing autographs.

Malevolent turned and sneered at Loco standing behind the turntables. Loco ignored his best friend's feelings and swaggered toward him, bumping fists. Malevolent had to play it cool but couldn't control himself. The best friends gave a hostile bump of their fists.

"I've got it in for your motherfucking ass!" Malevolent aggressively embraced Loco and gritted his teeth. Loco shoved him away and laughed it off. Malevolent then threw the mic on the stage, startling the crowd. Fans covered their ears because of the deafening sound as they witnessed him swaggering away.

"I don't know what's wrong with him!" Loco mouthed to himself. He noticed he stood before the audience as they applauded him. He picked up the mic, apologizing for Malevolent dropping it. He reassured the fans it was an accident. They cheered, followed by more black roses and even some red roses thrown on the stage. "Thank you, everyone!"

As Malevolent stormed his way through the crowd, his heart raced in his chest. He sensed that this night wasn't going to go right and felt the tension. Maybe he should leave and go see Portia. She was home, cooking or watching television. Malevolent knew she was a real homebody and didn't go out much, only to attend her piano classes. Portia wasn't a party girl, and in this business, there were nothing but party girls who had nothing going for themselves. All they did was party in clubs, hook up with hustlers, rappers, athletes, or some other well-to-do gentleman.

He knew he wasn't supposed to act like this because

these people came to support him, but he had to keep his cool. He stepped onto a large balcony where there weren't many people. Sparkling skyscrapers sprawled before his eyes, and he glared at the windows of the buildings, wondering if the people inside had troubles despite their success. He smelled a rose-scented fragrance in the air and turned to see a middle-aged woman approaching him with a grimace. Malevolent recognized her: her ebony hair now had gray streaks, and fine lines marked her face. She was still small in stature.

Malevolent, already pissed off, had to deal with the woman who caused him a lifetime of misery. She brought him a bull-shit story. *"What happened? Did Rico Suave leave her for an even younger woman?"*

Malevolent blocked the negative feelings from his mind because he already had enough tension. He didn't want to screw up his night. He would try to have a good time as best he could. He grimaced at his estranged mother and beckoned her. Rosa took baby steps toward her son with her eyes fixed on him. But Malevolent focused on the beautiful New York skyscrapers, waiting for her to say something so he could give her a good tongue-lashing. He decided to let it go because life's too short. Malevolent wasn't sure he even loved his mother. She wasn't around after his father died. All these years, Rosa had been absent from her son's life, and all Malevolent had was his father's side of the family to help raise him. His mother kept her distance, gawking at the jaw-dropping glamorous buildings.

Just being alone with her on this enormous balcony, he had the crazy thought about tossing her off and letting her fall to her death. He wasn't going to prison on the likes of her. The best thing to do was to let it go. It was his father's fault for pulling the trigger; he hadn't thought about how his demise would affect Malevolent in the long run. He turned fiery red in the face because his father was selfish.

"What do you want? Say something!" he glared at her with rage.

"I'm sorry, son," Rosa apologized for the damage she caused by breaking up their family. Rosa inched her way toward her son, but he backed away.

"I'm sorry too! I'm sorry I had both of you as parents!" Malevolent's rage caused his guests and colleagues to take notice. Benji rushed to his side, trying to calm him down.

"Are you alright, Mal?" Benji patted him on the shoulder.

"Can we talk about this some other time? I'm right in the middle of my celebration!" Malevolent pointed towards the exit as his mother tearfully left the venue. More of Malevolent's colleagues consoled him, escorting him to the lounge area.

"Alright, everyone, the party will proceed. Sorry for that disturbance. Malevolent will be signing more autographs and taking photos soon. Thank you for your cooperation," Benji said.

At a long fancy table an hour later, Malevolent sat in a chair signing autographs for some fans. He bumped fists with two male fans while a photograph was snapped. There was one with a pretty Asian girl in her late teens; another photo was taken, and more and more fans greeted him. The line stretched out into the hall and down the staircase. Benji would let him know how many people had come out to the event. Loco was on the other side of the table, chatting with whoever it was he was talking to. They didn't look important—just some thugs from any street corner in the hood. Loco always surrounded himself with losers.

These guys had nothing going for themselves but dreams of becoming hip-hop sensations or being associated with one. Another reason Loco and Malevolent's friendship wasn't as strong as it should've been was because of Loco's stupid associations with bums. Malevolent noticed Loco talking to a gentleman who seemed like someone from the underworld. Anyone would assume he was a pimp or drug dealer. A handsome, tall Latino ruffian, early forties, dressed in black street attire, cornrow styled hair, swaggered towards Malevolent. This menacing gentleman shook his hand, congratulating him on his success. He went by the street name, Tigre, and illegal activities was his business. He was the man who knew celebrities, and they knew him because he was one in his own right.

In the VIP section minutes later, five bottle girls, dressed in revealing outfits, serving sparkling alcoholic drinks to Malevolent, Loco, Tigre, and guests, clinking wine glasses to celebrate. They chatted among themselves as a hip-hop radio host approached the area. They wanted to get an interview with both MC Malevolent and DJ Loco as he leaned on the long leather sofa. Tigre and his entourage respectfully excused themselves, allowing the radio host to sit in the recliner. Another hip-hop radio host, STR-Eight, an African-American man in his mid-thirties, held a microphone in his hand. When the show went live, the sound of a muscle car engine roaring blared in the background. STR-8 loved muscle cars and fast cars in general and drove one himself, just like Malevolent.

"Welcome to the STR-8 show! I'm here to congratulate and celebrate the success of this hip-hop duo from Rego Park, Queens. Give it up for MC Malevolent and DJ Loco!" he shouted. People in the VIP section and others outside could hear the interview as they applauded.

"Congratulations on the new album 'Mourning Rose,'" STR-8 hollered, his voice muffled in the mic. "How does it feel to know that you made it happen?" The radio host shoved the microphone into Malevolent's face.

"Life is good! I'm blessed. I've got my family, my main man Loco, and just blessings all around," Malevolent stretched his arm along the top of the sofa. He told the truth about his blessings but played it off for the interview; he and Loco weren't cool for now.

As STR-8 peppered him with questions about his life and how everything transpired, he didn't make any eye contact with Loco. From the corner of his eye, he saw Loco acting the same way as he had during their prior radio interview. Malevolent hoped Loco wouldn't expose Portia during this one; that would be another embarrassment. When it was Loco's time to speak, he focused on the album. Surprisingly, he spoke about creating beats and working with his best friend, bragging about their future. Malevolent then gawked at a group of girls, waiting for an autograph and a photo with him. In a black, tight-fitting jumper, Portia waited in line right behind the girls. Malevolent leaned forward and glanced over both shoulders as the interview was still being conducted. He didn't want to excuse himself and dash to Portia; that would be unprofessional. His heart raced in his chest as he slowly smiled, relieved his love showed up to the party. And Portia looked beautiful; certain parts of his body began to get excited. *"Shit! Portia looks so good in that jumper!"* he thought, trying to stay focused.

After the party, he wanted to spend the rest of the night with his girl. This event would probably stretch into the early morning hours. DJ SRT-8 then stuck the microphone in Malevolent's face.

"So, Malevolent, I love 'Boom! In the Night!'"

"Thank you, STR-8," Malevolent nodded.

"The piano was cool on that track," the interviewer said.

"That's thanks to my girl, Portia," Malevolent replied, looking in her direction. DJ SRT-8 noticed the direction of his eyes, which also caught Loco's attention. His jaw dropped as he saw Portia dressed like a fashion plate, even better than the girls she stood behind. Loco turned red in the face, watching Malevolent smile as he beckoned Portia to approach the VIP section. He and Portia made eye contact; he could tell she was nervous.

Portia rushed towards her lover, sitting beside him. Malevolent wrapped his arms around her, kissing her on the cheek. He introduced his pride and joy to DJ SRT-8, who shook Portia's hand and peppered her with questions. Loco sat there, watching Malevolent loving on Portia. Loco eyed her from head to toe while his heart raced and a bulge in his pants emerged. He knew these two were going to get it on after the party. On top of that, Portia's glistening ring caught Loco's eye, and he wanted it. Slouching in his posture, Loco's frowned and then focused his eyes in the other direction. The interview continued while the radio host asked Portia more questions as she didn't make eye contact with Loco as well.

On the glamorous New York City balcony, minutes later with the sparkling buildings in the background, Malevolent and Portia kissed passionately, wrapped in each other's arms. They were so deep in their love, it was as if they were about to get it. A warm breeze blew through Portia's medium-length hair as Malevolent ran his fingers through it. They didn't care who saw and even forgot, they were at this party. And all they saw was each other, but someone else saw them. Loco crept in the background, drinking from a paper cup, and witnessing the lovers in each other's arms. His heart throbbed in his chest, face turn fiery red, he crumpled the paper cup in his hand. He wanted to throw the cup at Malevolent, but what good would that do? He had something else in mind. "He wanted that ring!"

CHAPTER TWENTY-TWO

Towering brick buildings stood majestically on Manhattan's lower east side alongside the FDR Drive and other urban infrastructures. Regardless of where anyone drove in Manhattan, there was always traffic. On this dismal morning, Malevolent drove his muscle car into the parking lot adjacent to these apartments. He pulled into a space and shut down the monstrous engine. He hopped from the driver's seat, looking around, hoping no one would attempt to steal his vehicle. If they did, he'd get another one.

He swaggered up the block, noticing some thugs hanging outside the building, doing absolutely nothing.

"Holy shit! Malevolent, what's up?" a short hooligan bumped fists with Malevolent as the group gave him a fist-bump greeting.

"Yo, Malevolent! I love 'Boom! In the Night!'" a bald-headed ruffian puffed on a cigarette.

"Thanks, man," Malevolent smiled and rushed into the building.

"Malevolent, what brings you to this neck of the hood?"

the bald ruffian asked as he took the last puff of his smoke. He threw the bud on the ground, mashing the light out with his foot.

"My mother lives here. On the fourteenth floor."

"Alright, cool! Keep making that good music," the ruffian complimented.

Malevolent nodded and swaggered to the elevator. He pressed the elevator button, waiting for the elevator to come the ground floor. And it did. The door slowly opened as Malevolent hopped in. He pressed the fourteenth elevator button as the door was about to close, a hand reached in and forcing it open. A dingy, raggedy urban-clad gentleman, average height, mid-twenties, stood in front of Malevolent. He didn't make eye contact with this rapper. Malevolent's heart pumped in his chest as balls of sweat formed on his forehead. He had no weapons on him, so the only thing he had was his fists. He clenched his hands into fists, ready for what was to come. Then the elevator rose up the upper floors, stopping at the eight floor and the door widened as the unkempt gentleman exited. Then Malevolent pressed the fourteenth elevator button as the door closed again. The elevator ascended to the upper floor, Malevolent did the sign of the cross. Finally, it reached the fourteenth floor and the heavy steel door widened. Malevolent swaggered down a well-lit hallway, where there was an echo in the long hallway. He approached apartment door fourteen-thirteen, ringing the doorbell and heard his song "Boom! In the Night!" playing. Malevolent shook his head and wondered after all these years she has now decided to come back into his life. Is she after money? Probably so, if that's the case then she won't get a dime. But, the visit to his mother's was so he could get some closure. And then maybe, they could rebuild their bond. Then the lock on the door clicked as it swung open as a seventeen-year-old, kid, dressed in the latest street styled urban wear, his jaw dropped.

"Holy shit! Malevolent! What the fuck!" the young teen, obviously a fan, exclaimed. Malevolent smiled at the young kid, who then bumped fists with him.

"Mom!" the seventeen-year-old hollered. "Come in! Come in!"

Without hesitation, Malevolent stepped into the apartment, glancing over both shoulders, hoping he was in the right place. "Does Rosa live here?"

"Yes, she does," the teenager gasped. "Are you banging my mom?"

"No! Rosa's my mother," Malevolent snickered.

Rosa rushed into the living room, spotting her estranged son standing there with Aaron, her other son. She embraced Alejandro and then Aaron as well. Aaron couldn't figure out what this was all about. While Alejandro was still embraced in his mother's arms, he noticed Aaron's baby and grade school photos, along with an eight-by-ten wedding photo of Rosa and Claudio. Malevolent's heart dropped upon seeing the picture of his mother with another man. He wanted to curse her to hell and back. He closed his eyes, trying to fight back the tears that would cascade down his face. But no success; those watery droplets slid down his cheeks as he sobbed. Rosa tightened her embrace around her firstborn while tears flowed from her eyes as well. Malevolent didn't want to start crying like a baby in front of a fan's face. But this fan was his stepbrother, and he was meeting him for the first time. He had to let that go as he and his mother sat on the couch.

In the midst of Rosa explaining her side of the story regarding the past events, Malevolent made eye contact with the photo of her new family. His heart pumped in his chest, and his face turned fiery red. "I'm not angry that you and Pop broke up! It's the way you did it! He blew himself away!"

Aaron, lounged in a recliner across from his mother and new stepbrother, arching his eyebrows and gasping as he heard about Malevolent's father. He glared at his mother, thinking, "Why would she do something so stupid? How could she be so thoughtless and selfish?" Now, Aaron understood Malevolent's album "Mourning Rose," especially "Boom! In the Night," where he heard his stepbrother recount the arguments his father had with their mother because she wouldn't come back to them. And word was, Rosa was three weeks pregnant with Aaron. "What the fuck! I was already three weeks in the womb when this shit went down!" Aaron stood from the recliner and paced on the carpet, becoming teary-eyed.

"Do you know he could've been here to blow us away?"

"No! No such thing crossed my mind, bro!" Malevolent shook his head.

"It could've happened!"

"And it didn't!" Malevolent embraced Aaron, who cried in his arms.

Keys jingled at the apartment door as the locks clicked, and the hinges squeaked as the door opened. Stomping in was Claudio Rivera, still handsome, with matured salt-and-pepper hair, who noticed Aaron and the somewhat older guy—maybe another one of his neighborhood friends. Rosa rushed to her husband, giving him a kiss on the cheek and trying to escort him into the kitchen. Claudio was determined to know who this kid was.

"Alejandro!" Claudio squinted his eyes. Malevolent didn't respond to his born given-name and to the man who destroyed his life as a child. Claudio took baby steps towards him, extending his hand for a shake. Malevolent and Aaron took a couple of steps away from him. Aaron glared at his father, balling his hands into fists. He wanted so badly to slug his own father, tears streaming down his face as he stormed out of the apartment, aggressively thrusting the door open.

"Aaron! What happened?" Claudio gasped in wonder. He looked at Rosa, shrugging his shoulders, then to Malevolent.

"You know exactly what the fuck happened!" Malevolent rushed out of the apartment.

Underneath the cloudy skies that proceeded, watery-eyed Aaron pushed the heavy apartment door open with all his might, causing the glass window to shatter. Malevolent heard the loud crash, dashing to the first floor. His jaw dropped, noticing cracks in the glass, hoping Aaron wouldn't get in serious trouble for the damages. Malevolent hurried away from the building and down the street. Hoping he wouldn't face any consequences either.

"Aaron!" he cried out to his stepbrother. Malevolent was determined to make things right with this young man who wasn't only a fan but his brother. He wouldn't allow the past to affect their relationship or their future. He blocked Aaron's path, placing his arm around him.

"It's going to be alright, man," Malevolent embraced him while Aaron cried like a baby. Aaron wrestled out of his brother's embrace.

"I wouldn't blame you if you left! You're probably here for just one visit!" Aaron said.

"I'm not here for a visit!" Malevolent differed.

"So, what then?" Aaron shrugged.

"I'm here to get to know you, man. Mom told me I had a baby brother, so I came to bond with you." Malevolent attempting to bump fists with Aaron. Aaron wondered how they could have a good relationship with a dirty past. Now, he felt like shit, just like Malevolent did because of it. Their past haunted them both. Malevolent didn't want Aaron to be affected by their mother's adulterous behavior, but Aaron couldn't get over it. He figured he would need to speak to a counselor or a close friend. The young guys around Aaron's neighborhood were cutthroat and wouldn't spit on you if you were on fire.

"So, how do you spend your time?" Malevolent asked.

"I listen to music and always wanted to become a DJ," Aaron smirked.

"Really?" Malevolent smiled as a thought came to mind. Since he and Loco weren't on good terms, maybe he could have his little brother as his new DJ. First, Malevolent would have to put him to the test.

"DJ Loco is my favorite!" Aaron cackled.

"Are you sure about that?" Malevolent shook his head in disappointment. "What other DJs do you admire?"

"DJ Premier, DJ Khaled, DJ Red Alert, Kid Capri, Funk Master Flex, Sir Jinx from the West Coast, and others," Aaron counted the DJs on his fingers like a child learning to count.

"That's cool. You listen to a lot of old-school hip-hop?" Malevolent bumped fists with Aaron.

"Yes. What's up with you and Loco?" Aaron glared at his brother directly. Malevolent didn't want to tell him that he was now going through a similar situation as their mother.

"It's..." Malevolent attempted to articulate his words, figuring out the best way to tell Aaron. "It's some shit."

"What shit?"

"Some shit," Malevolent focusing his eyes on the enormous buildings and the FDR Drive.

"Portia's your girl?" Aaron asked.

"Yeah. Portia's my heart," Malevolent replied.

"I saw the interview with you and Loco with DJ STR-8. Is he trying to steal your girl?"

"Seems that way," Malevolent exhaled.

"What are you going to do about it?" Aaron shrugged.

"What do you mean... what am I going to do about it?" Malevolent laughed it off.

"I would fuck him up," Aaron cracked his knuckles.

"What do you mean, 'fuck him up'?" Malevolent asked.

"Are you scared?" Aaron punching his fist in the palm of his hand.

"Nah. I'm not scared. I've got a career to think about. I've got my whole life ahead of me. I've got plans," Malevolent scratched his head.

"What are you going to do if he comes at you?" Aaron asked.

"Loco isn't going to do anything," Malevolent looked away.

"You don't know that," Aaron lifted up his hoodie, revealing a nine-millimeter gun in his waistband.

"Where the fuck did you get that?" Malevolent gasped, looking around, hoping no one was watching them, especially the boys in blue.

"Don't worry about that! You need to worry about your safety." Aaron then hid the firearm under his hoodie.

"You're a kid, Aaron," Malevolent said.

"I'm a man," Aaron patted his chest.

"Do you think a gun is going to help you in life?" Malevolent asked.

"It'll save it," Aaron responded.

"And you'll probably take a life. And then serve life," Malevolent added. "Are you serious about music or what?"

"Yes, I'm serious," Aaron shrugged.

"Then get rid of that shit," Malevolent looked at the waistband where he hid his firearm.

"No," Aaron shook his head.

Malevolent refrained from telling this kid what to do—after all, he just met him. He scratched his head, figuring out how to work with his stepbrother.

"Bet. Come down to the studio, show me your turntable skills, and I'll hook you up," Malevolent offered.

"Are you serious, bro?" Aaron leaned forward, his jaw dropping open.

"As a heart attack," Malevolent inhaled mucus through his nostrils and spat the yellow saliva on the cement. "Now, get rid of the piece!"

"No," Aaron shook his head.

"I'm giving you an opportunity that could change your life forever," Malevolent said.

"No, I'm not getting rid of my shit. You're my favorite rapper, and I found out we're brothers, but still," Aaron turned away from Malevolent and looking in the other direction.

"I apologize for telling you how to live your life. Are you still going to take this opportunity?" Malevolent got in his younger brother's face.

"Yes, I'm down," Aaron smirked. The brothers bumped fists as they swaggered toward the apartment buildings.

"And I've got my man who raps, MC Chance. He's real dope!"

"Seriously?" Malevolent asked.

"Like a heart attack," Aaron replied. They both laughed.

"Do you know what would be a good name for you, Aaron?" Malevolent patted him on the back.

"What would be a catchy name?" Aaron asked.

"DJ Knucklehead," Malevolent snickered.

"Seriously! That's not bad!" Aaron laughed.

CHAPTER TWENTY-THREE

A reddish-lit steel caged elevator ascended to the upper floors of an old, dark warehouse. Loco rode this enormous lift multiple times before and accompanied by a short- dread-locked ruffian with tattoos and piercings. As usual, they didn't exchange any words because they had no business dealings. All they did was nod. Loco sported a black hoodie, black jeans, and sneakers and puffed out his chest. His eyes shifted from left to right, and glanced over his shoulders while this elevator ruffian proceeded to do his duty. While the elevator continued to the upper floors, the hellish red glow faded in and out passing each level. Then it halted to the top floor as the ruffian elevator operator opened the caged doors. The loud, rattling sound echoed throughout the entire building that scared Loco even though he had to play it cool. He stepped off and to gray cemented floor, as the rattling elevator closed its doors and descended to the lower floor. Loco's been to this place before and always had to show that he had no fear. Still, he glanced over his shoulders, noticing no one was in the lobby. He fixed his eyes on the ceiling with its dimmed lighting, some flickered, while a couple were burnt-out. There were some rusted pipes along the walls, old tires, thick link chains that swung above his head and machinery for automobiles. While, Loco displayed bravery in his stride, he hoped no one would ambush him. When Loco was a teenager, he always associated with other peers who were drop-outs, got suspended or participated in illegal activities which caused Loco wanting to be a part of the action. Rap music reverberating in the distance and became familiar to him. "Machete" blasting. "Oh, shit!" Loco thought. They really like Malevolent's work. But, it's really my work because I'm the genius behind it all." For a minute, Loco had another reason to resent Malevolent because he would get the credit and he'd be dwindling in the background. Never mind that, Loco had to focus on not getting the shit beat out of him, swaggering along this murky floor. He kept a leveled head as he stumbled upon a familiar corridor with an intense reddish lighting. Loco approached the end of it, sensing as if he were about to enter hell. Balls of sweat surfaced on his forehead as he quickly wiped it away. Then a shoulder-tiger tattooed, stocky, security guard, Ray, mid-forties, appeared out of nowhere, poking out his chest.

"Holy shit! Loco what's up," the guard fist bumped Loco. Ray acted like a groupie, smiling from ear to ear.

"What's up?" Loco returned the gesture. He loved receiving acknowledgment from people that he was familiar with. Ray wasted no time, well aware of Loco's visits, escorting him down another even darker and longer corridor. Loco's heart raced in his chest and knew what was down this hallway. But, he still didn't know what danger he would encounter. Then another reddish glow brightened the area. Loco looked over his shoulders again, with his eyes shifting in his head. His heart couldn't stop racing, but he had to take a deep breath and slow down his heartbeat.

Both men approached a steel door as Ray rang the buzzer.

"Quien es?" a masculine voice from the other side asked in Spanish. "Ray!"

Loco noticed a security camera above the door. Then metal locks on the heavy door clanked as a skinny, drowsy-eyed, gentleman by the name Snooze, mid-fifties, with faded tattaoos, opened it, puffing on a cigarette.

“What?” Snooze asked, noticing Ray with a someone that he didn’t recognize.

“Look at what the cat dragged in,” Ray cackled, pointing at Loco.

“What’s going on, Loco?” Snooze’s eyed widened as if he just hit the number. He bumped Loco’s fist.

“What’s up, Snooze!” Loco returned the gesture.

“How are you doing, man? I’m looking forward to that album with you and Malevolent,” Loco smiled. Then a short, weird, girl, early-twenties, red braided hair approach Snooze’s side. She frowned at Loco and eyed him from head to toe. He couldn't stand it when this girl gave him dirty looks. Every time he would visit, he was always met with this red-headed broad’s glares. She probably wanted to fuck him because he was a well-known DJ. Loco and Snooze swaggered into the room as the red-headed woman closed the heavy door.

Upon Loco and Snooze's entrance into the back room, a crimson luminescence illuminated the entire environment. Following this, he took a breath and discerned the smell which was a nutty, savory aroma similar to corn chips and it smelled like a zoo. Loco knew there was a wild animal, but still toughened up. He and Snooze noticed several tattooed ruffians counting money by hand or in the counting machine. Directly behind them was an enormous, thick glass with a six-hundred-pound, tiger, growling, and pacing with a thick link chain around its neck. Anyone could tell that this beast was ready for its meal. Loco couldn't stop his rapid heartbeat because anything could happen to him in a place like this. Upon entering into this sophisticated lounge, one observed a substantial flat-panel television affixed to the wall, a pool table suspended beneath a Tiffany lamp, luxurious black cherry wood leather seating, and an impressive black cherry wood bar. Furthermore, a more expansive lounge space was furnished with an elegant leather sofa, a recliner, a loveseat, ornate chairs, a coffee table, and wall adornments featuring imagery of the Dominican Republic, tigers, automobiles, and additional subjects.

"Look who's here, Tigre," Snooze hollered over the loud rap music.

"Loco, what's up!" Tigre stood from his recliner, bumping fists with him.

"Chillin! Chillin'!" Loco responded.

"Sit down! Bring two beers sweetheart!" Tigre snapped his finger, getting a young pretty girl's attention. Loco relaxed on the black sofa with the glass case behind of Tigre's exotic cat. The large striped cat growled, pacing in its man-made habitat. Loco constantly glanced over his shoulder at the animal. "Don't worry, Loco! You're not on the menu!" Tigre and his crew cackled. Tigre and Loco go way back to elementary school. Tigre's birth name: Antonio Torres was a raised in the gritty streets since a kid. He and Loco reminisced about playing hooky in the fifth and sixth grade. Their teacher called their mothers to find out why they weren't in school for days. Come to find out, Loco was hanging out with Tigre the entire time, playing video games, watching movies, and ordering fast food. When Loco got home after three, he acted as if he had a regular school day. When Mrs. Porter found out, she raised hell and wanted to tell Loco's father about his son's behavior. But his father didn't care because he was busy chasing other women. That's the reason why Loco never had fatherly supervision. On the other hand, Tigre's upbringing was different. His family didn't care, coming from a broken home where his drunk mother was always stretched out in bed and father wasn't anywhere to be found. He had to find his own way in the world and now, he's a kingpin with an army in the thousands. Rap music continued to blast from a speaker in the corner of the lounge room as "Roses Are Black" played. Then the young girl set a silver ice bucket with two fancy beer bottles and napkins. Tigre was a real Malevolent fan and felt that it was a privilege to know this rap duo personally. His entourage, mostly men and a few women gathered around with goo-goo eyes because of this celebrity DJ before them. Tigre looked forward to Malevolent and Loco's concerts, music and more music videos. He also gave his condolences to Loco because he lost someone very dear to him. Furthermore, Tigre also admired the black rose featured on the album cover. Loco recounted to Tigre and his associates about he and Malevolent's shared history in Rego Park, their sustained friendship, and voiced doubts concerning their prospects in the music industry.

"I heard that you and Mal are fighting over some bitch named, Portia," a slender ruffian insulted with a puff of his cigarette, releasing smoke into the air. Tigre and Loco sprung from their seats, knocking him to the floor and stomping him. Tigre grabbed the skinny guy by the collar, hurling a punch to his face which he plummeted to the floor again. Loco then stomped him again and Tigre and his entourage hauled him out of the lounge.

“I apologize for that, man” Tigre bumped fists with Loco.

“That’s not your fault! Fools don’t know how to shut the fuck up,” Loco sat on the sofa, stretching his arm along the back. The men immediately laughed about the incident and immediately changed the subject. Loco dove deeper into the tale of he and Malevolent who had their hearts set on the same woman. Tigre couldn't understand why Loco would fight with his best friend over some woman.

“Portia’s not some side chick hanging around the studio,” Loco explained. She was a college student who came from a good family, respectful, and she was a classical pianist who was a great artist. At first Tigre and his entourage thought Portia was some groupie willing to fuck Malevolent and Loco, and every rapper that crossed her path. But, not so. Portia had a bright future in the classical music world. Loco also added that, he had a girlfriend who died of cancer, a talented violinist who was bound for greatness. Tigre and posse's eyes widened hearing the story of Loco's tragic tale.

"I need some heat," Loco glared at Tigre in the eye. He glanced at the striped cat in the glass case over his shoulder, devouring a raw piece of meat.

Moments later, Loco grasped a nine-millimeter firearm, aiming it at a gun target. He fired several shots into the middle of it. Tigre's eye widened, noticing that Loco meant business as a smirk surfaced on his face and asked for more weapons. For a second, Tigre became somewhat fearful of this man he admired, but willingly showed more of his weaponry display. He and Loco swaggered to a security door with a passcode. Tigre keyed in the number that unlocked the door, pulling it opened. Then there another reddish gleam shone upon Loco's face, noticing semi-automatic pistols, rifles, machine guns, machetes, and other weapons mounted on the walls and on a long fancy table. Loco grabbed the Colombian machete from the wall. He waved the large blade in the air, hearing its sound in the air just like in the movies. Tigre stood back, allowing him to browse.

"You could try that out if you like," he offered.

"Nah. That's alright. I'd rather have a pistol," Loco placed the blade back on the wall. Tigre nodded and still giving him time to make his decision.

Loco browsed the red room, grasping a semi-automatic rifle. He wanted to tell Tigre what this was for, but kept his mouth shut. He knew if something serious was to become of his plans he wouldn't snitch on Tigre. Exquisite jewelry was showcased within the glass display case, accompanied by high-end designer apparel arranged on the clothing racks, alongside an array of fashionable footwear and athletic shoes. Loco set the rifle down on the table and moved towards the jewelry case, his attention drawn to the sparkling possessions. The ruby red ring possessed its own distinct radiance, setting it apart from the other glittering jewels.

"How much is that ring?" Loco pointed at the sparkling jewel.

"I can give it to you for a thousand," Tigre stood behind the glass case as if he were a salesperson in an actual jewelry store. He used the key to open up the glass case, presenting the ring to Loco.

"Here you go," Loco smiled. "Is that for Portia?"

"Yes, it is," Loco nodded. He inspected the ring to make sure it was real.

"Don't worry, Loco. It's real," Tigre chuckled.

"I just want to give her the best," Loco said.

"You're dead serious about Portia, aren't you?" Tigre asked.

"Yes," Loco answered.

"What are you planning on doing?" Tigre arched an eyebrow.

"Just watch the news," Loco replied with a fiendish smile on his face.

CHAPTER TWENTY-FOUR

Days later, in the nocturnal hours within a murky recording studio, Malevolent and Aaron were situated at the soundboard, monitoring MC Chance, a rapper from the Lower East Side. Aaron and Chance were childhood companions, residing in adjacent buildings and sharing an educational journey from kindergarten through high school. Chance spewed obscene lyrics into the pop-filtered retro microphone while Malevolent, Aaron, Benji, and two studio engineers listened to this upcoming star. In the background, an entourage of twenty-four tagalongs from the Lower East Side rooted for him. Malevolent gave a thumbs-up to Chance and patted Aaron on the back for a job well done. He almost forgot about the drama with Loco. Right now, he focused on building a relationship with his brother Aaron, producing this new talent MC Chance, and eventually, marrying Portia. He and Loco were a duo with an album ready to drop. He couldn't fathom why Loco would mess up their success. They were supposed to be in this studio right now, creating more music, discovering new artists, and making lots of money. The way things were going between him and Loco, they could kiss their careers goodbye. Not only was Malevolent concerned about this dispute, but Benji was as well. He wanted them to settle their differences because he had booked interviews, music videos, guest appearances, and the opening act for Joey Jose's concert.

Benji asked Malevolent if he had heard from Loco since their altercation at the album release party. Malevolent shook his head, keeping his eyes fixed on Chance in the booth. He didn't utter another word. For some strange reason, he noticed Chance's musical potential and almost believed he rhymed better than he did. If that were the case, then so be it. He knew he shouldn't downplay his work and wasn't going to say anything to Benji about it. Benji put a lot of effort into getting MC Malevolent and DJ Loco's music out into the world.

Anyway, MC Chance's music would make the crowd dance while Malevolent's music was trauma. "Why didn't he seek counseling for his childhood past?" he thought. He glanced over his shoulder at Chance's neighborhood entourage from the Lower East Side, nodding their heads to the music. One of Chance's friend's bumped fists with Aaron, enjoying his musical session. Throughout this joyous music, Malevolent noticed an hour glass shaped woman, wearing black sweat pants and a hoodie with a designer logo, heaving a large musical instrument in a case. She wore sunglasses even though it was night. He still didn't recognize this woman. "Was she one of Chance's female friends? Or better yet, a groupie hoping to be arm candy. Malevolent rose from the recliner to see who she was? As he swaggered closer, this woman removed the dark glasses from her eyes. Malevolent gasped as his eyes widened, seeing the black and blue ring around Jazzy's eye. "Jazzy?" he couldn't fathom her condition. Then it hit him. *"Did Loco do this to her? What the fuck!"* all sorts of thoughts of beating the shit out of him came to mind.

"Is Loco here?" Jazzy whined, tears welling in her bruised eyes as they streamed down her face. Malevolent knew that this monster had done something terrible to her. He gently grabbed Jazzy by the arm, escorting her to the lobby of the building. He didn't want to be rude and dismiss her like Loco did. He knew he had to be in the recording session, but Benji and Aaron were there. Aaron had a lot of potential, and he and Benji seemed to hit it off right from the start.

Malevolent and Jazzy entered the dimly lit lobby and sat on the cushioned sofa. The receptionist's desk was right in front of them while Tony was striking keys on the computer at his lit desk. Malevolent proceeded to gawk at Jazzy's face, lifting her chin to get a good look at her blackened eye.

"Did he?" Malevolent's face slowly turned red. Jazzy turned away from him, sobbing and wrapping her arms around the enormous cello in a gray case. *"When did she start playing the cello? Does she know how to play a musical instrument?"* Malevolent asked himself. He didn't want to come off as insensitive about this instrument that she must've paid a fortune for.

As Jazzy placed her head down, hugging her instrument, Malevolent strutted over to the receptionist for some Kleenex. He heard the bubbling sounds of mucus as she cried, and he knew this was bad. "Loco, that motherfucker!"

He swaggered back to Jazzy, shoving the box of tissues in her face. "Here." Jazzy snatched a tissue from the box, wiping her eyes. He wondered if he should ask Jazzy in detail what happened. And what was he going to do about it? It's not like Jazzy was his girl. Questions popped into his mind along with even more questions, but he couldn't do anything about it. Malevolent eased his body onto the sofa next to Jazzy. She continued to sob, grabbing more tissues from the box. Each tear that fell represented the many times Loco hurt her. Then she blew her nose into the tissue. Malevolent cringed at the disgusting sound. He focused his eyes in the other direction. Jazzy inhaled and turned to him.

"I guess you're wondering why I'm carrying this cello with me? Maybe if I knew how to play a musical instrument, Loco would love me. Or somebody would love me," Jazzy's voice quivered. Malevolent couldn't bear to look at her in her condition. He had to get her out of there because Portia was on her way to the studio.

"I'll call you an Uber," Malevolent punched in the numbers for a car service on his cellphone.

"Aren't you going to ask me what happened?" Jazzy cried. Malevolent had never been cold-hearted to a woman in his life. He was acting like Loco.

"Your ride will be here in a minute," Malevolent said, ending the call.

"Loco beat the shit out of me! He wanted me to drive a wedge between you and Portia! He's in love with Portia!" Jazzy whined, sobbing again.

"I know all that shit," Malevolent stood up from the sofa. Headlights from a slowly driving vehicle reflected on the glass door. "That was mad quick! Your Uber is here," he hauled the hefty cello case toward the car as Jazzy followed him.

"Buzz me out, Tony!" Malevolent called out. The entrance doors buzzed, and he pushed the door open, aggressively heaving the cello case toward the car. He sensed Jazzy sprinting up to him. Malevolent thrust opened the back passenger's side door and threw the classical instrument into the back seat. "Fuck!" Malevolent hollered, holding the door open for her to get in.

"What are you doing? That cello cost me twenty-four hundred, Malevolent!" Jazzy shoved him.

"Maybe you should've thought about that before you spent nineteen grand on your Brazilian ass lift! Good luck with your symphony endeavors!" Malevolent swaggered away from Jazzy as she stood with the car door open. He didn't look back as he hurried back to the studio. The only things he heard were the driver telling her to get into the Uber, the door closing, and the vehicle driving away.

He approached the entrance, pounding on the glass. The door buzzed, and Malevolent entered the building. He wanted to glance back at the Uber driving away but kept his focus on getting back into the recording studio. He gave a thumbs-up to Tony for staying late nights, allowing him in and out of the building. He acted as if he owned the place, but someday he would own a recording studio. Right now, he had to get back to the session.

Minutes later, Malevolent trotted to the recording studio, where he didn't hear any music. Chance wasn't rhyming; the only sounds came from Chance's neighborhood entourage praising him. He stood in the background, noticing this new rap star and feeling a bit envious. There was no reason for Malevolent to feel threatened; he had a beautiful rap album coming out with controversial subject matters. He had discovered a new artist, MC Chance, who was a skilled rapper with a good producer—Malevolent himself.

He swaggered further into the recording studio, apologizing for the interruption. Even though he missed the last half of Chance's session, all he had to do was play it back and make some adjustments. Chance's neighborhood fans clamored, making it impossible for Malevolent to hear himself talk or even think.

"What's going on with Jazzy?" Benji asked in his ear.

"I don't know—some bullshit about her circumstances!" Malevolent shrugged and bumped fists with Chance. "Great work so far!"

In a matter of no time, MC Chance was in the recording

studio, working on another musical track, headsets and all, with his friends from the community fixated on him. Malevolent and Aaron swayed in their recliners, bobbing their heads to the boom-bap beat. Benji was alongside them, jotting down notes on maneuvering MC Malevolent and DJ Loco (the hip-hop duo) and MC Chance (a solo artist). Everyone applauded this new artist's track. Suddenly, the ceiling lights flickered and then stopped while no one thought anything of it and continued with the music session.

The ceiling lights flickered again and then shut off. Complete darkness enveloped the recording studio, accompanied by strange sounds.

"What the fuck! What happened to the power?" Malevolent shouted through the murky studio. The power came back on, lights and recording studio equipment resuming. “Let me see what the problem is,” Benji excused himself from the soundboard.

Malevolent and everyone gasped. “Are you cool, little brother?” Malevolent bumped fists with Aaron.

“Yeah, I'm chilling,” Aaron rocked in his recliner.

“Cool,” Malevolent turned on the speakers inside the recording booth. “Chance, are you alright?”

“Yeah, I'm cool,” Chance gave a thumbs-up to Malevolent, Aaron, and his entourage who applauded for his well-being. Then, BOOM! The lights went out again.

"Holy shit!” one of Chance's cronies shouted. The lights came back on but kept flickering.

“What the fuck was that sound?” Malevolent shouted.

“It sounded like a gun,” Aaron's eyes widened.

“No fucking way!” Malevolent shook his head, hoping maybe a light bulb broke or something similar. Then another BOOM! Everyone looked at each other with fear in their eyes.

Malevolent eyed Chance in the tiny recording booth, who seemed alarmed and was looking around him.

"Yo! Those were gunshots!" Chance's voice echoed from the booth.

"I hope the fuck not! Benji!" Malevolent hollered from his recliner.

Again, complete darkness engulfed the recording studio as flashing lights and rapid gunfire erupted. Everyone clamored in the dark, seeking cover from the danger they couldn't see. The only things they saw were flashes from an unknown firearm. Malevolent ducked under the soundboard, grabbing his cellphone and using the light that shone from his screen. He focused the cellphone light in Aaron's face. His baby brother was right by his side, and Malevolent wanted to keep him there. The chaos proceeded with crashing glass, rummaging, cursing, screaming, and generalized horror overwhelming them. Malevolent feared he and Aaron were about to meet their demise. The best thing he could do was try to survive this situation. He put his finger to his mouth for them to keep quiet. He shut his cellphone, cutting off the light. The gunfire ceased while heavy feet pounding through the studio. The recording studio lights flickering, glass crashing, and the sound of a wall or something of the sort being kicked. "Yo! What are you doing please don't kill me!" Chance's voice muffled from the recording booth. Malevolent gasped as he opened his cellphone shining light.

"Who is that?" Aaron mouthed to his brother, shaking his head. Malevolent feared the worse and hoped that it wasn't who he thought it could be. Right now, he didn't have a firearm or anything to protect himself or his brother.

"What do they call you?" the familiar voice muffled from the recording booth.

MC Chance," his voice quivered.

“Where are you from?” the familiar voice asked in a stern tone.

“The Lower East Side,” Chance answered.

“Are you scared right now?” the unknown voice snickered.

“I don’t want to lose my life,” Chance took sharp breaths.

Malevolent heard the fear in this upcoming rapper’s voice. He then peeked up from under the soundboard, seeing Loco brandishing a semi-automatic rifle in Chance's face. Chance begged, plummeting to his knees. Malevolent saw the rage in Loco’s eyes from a distance. Evil could be seen from miles away. Malevolent crossed himself, praying to God to forgive him for his sins and to get him out of this dilemma. Maybe, it was his time to meet God and reunite with his father. He prayed for his career, success, Portia and all. The only way for him to get out of this, was to fight. He didn’t want to go to hell. He would experience fury between he and his former best friend. Malevolent felt bad about mistreating Jazzy as she tried to put her best foot forward. “God, forgive me,” he prayed. Malevolent ducked under the soundboard again, holding his head. “God please don’t let him do it! God, please, no! No!” BOOM!

"Malevolent! I know you're in here, motherfucker! So, come out and face me!" Malevolent’s heart raced in his chest and gestured for Aaron to remain still. He took a deep breath and rose from under the soundboard.

“I’m here, fool!” Malevolent put his hands in the air.

Loco brandished the semi-automatic rifle at Malevolent, moving towards him. “Do you have a gun on you?”

“I don’t have shit on me,” Malevolent’s hands trembled. “If you want to kill me, then do so. Portia is mine, plain and simple!”

“Portia’s mine!” Loco stepped closer, pointing the rifle at Malevolent’s forehead.

Malevolent continued to reach for the sky, trying to figure out what to do. But there was no way out of this. He didn't want to risk getting injured, nor did he want Aaron or anyone else in the studio to get hurt. Unfortunately, he noticed Aaron's neighborhood friends lying in a bloody pool. He hoped that his brother wouldn't do anything stupid, like intervene in this mess. Malevolent clenched his hand into a fist and punched Loco in the face. Stumbling, Loco managed to stay on his feet as the rifle fell out of his hands. Both men wrestled over the weapon as a gunshot rang out. Then another gunshot. "Alejandro!" a feminine voice cried out. Then another third shot rang out as complete darkness engulfed the studio, and clicking sounds echoed. The recording studio lights flickered back on, while Loco held the firearm, aiming at Portia. She laid in a bloody pool on the floor. Malevolent's heart sank as crawled to her and cradled her in his arms. He wept, watching blood flow from her stomach.

Loco looked at the rifle, disbelief flashing across his face. He paced back and forth, crying. Malevolent glared at Loco, who was acting stupid while holding the rifle. He wished there were bullets in the chamber so he could pull the hammer back, place it under his chin, and blow himself away. He cradled Portia as blood soaked into his shirt.

"I got this ring for Portia," Loco sobbed, holding the ring box in his hand. Malevolent slowly looked up and noticed the ruby red ring. It was similar to the platinum ring Portia had on her finger already.

"How the fuck were you going to go about that?" Malevolent gritted his teeth, his face turning fiery red as his heart pounded in his chest.

"Whichever one of us is still alive, gets to place the ring on her finger," Loco said with a sadistic smirk.

"What the fuck!" Malevolent's eyebrows arched.

"You and I fight to the death. If I send you to meet your maker, I'll place this ring on her finger as she goes into the next life," Loco's tears turned to a stern tone.

"What kind of sick shit is that?" Malevolent's voice quivered.

"Scared to challenge me? Come on, Mal," Loco screamed.

"What are you, stupid?" Malevolent said, kissing Portia's forehead. Suddenly, a glass bottle hit him in the head.

"What the fuck!" He felt warmth on top of his head, touched it, and saw blood on his hand. "Let's go! Bet!" Malevolent laid Portia on the floor. The two young men charged at each other, throwing punches. Loco landed an uppercut to Malevolent's chin, causing him to stumble. Malevolent, determined to keep his balance, exerted massive effort to take Loco down. They bounced around like boxers in the ring. Malevolent leaned in with a punch to Loco's face. Blood emerged from his nose and mouth as he spit it in Malevolent's face. Malevolent didn't stop there; he returned the favor, inhaling mucus through his nostrils and spitting in Loco's face.

Loco punched Malevolent in the face, causing blood to drip. Malevolent almost fell but managed to keep his balance. The former best friends hurled fists at one another, crashing into walls and creating large holes. They crashed through to the glass door of the larger studio that held instruments. They wrestled on the floor, chunks of glass beneath them. Loco wrapped his hands around Malevolent's neck, attempting to choke the life out of him. Loco's eyes bulged like a crazed cartoon character, teeth grinding, and his complexion turned hellish red.

Malevolent fought with all his strength to escape Loco's tight grip. He wished he had a machete in his hands; he would cut this asshole's head off. But for now, he had to fight with his bare hands. He kicked Loco in the nuts, crawling away to the other side of the studio, gasping. He saw Loco curled in a fetal position in agony. Malevolent stood to his feet, gasping for air. Then there was rumbling of a grand piano caught his attention. He turned, noticing the enormous instrument coming towards him as he immediately placed his hands on it. Loco's sweaty, wide-eyed demonic face trembled from the other end of the piano. Malevolent shoved the piano with all his might, caught between the wall and the instrument. He quickly dashed away from the wall and the gigantic instrument. He plummeted to the floor, witnessing the grand piano smash into the brick wall, damaging its beautiful wood, chunks scattering everywhere as the keys plinked. Loco shoved it towards Malevolent as he lay on the floor. Malevolent sprang to his feet, attempting to prevent Loco from injuring him.

The pushing resumed between the two men until the instrument slammed Loco's back against the brick wall. The tables had turned—Malevolent had the upper hand. He was determined to win his sweetheart's hand in marriage, even if she was gone. The ring on her finger that he had given would remain there; he wasn't going to let Loco have her. Loco's face shook, beads of sweat forming, and his eyes watering.

"Please don't kill me, Malevolent! What are you doing?" a sweet voice quivered. At the end of the piano, teary-eyed Portia struggled to keep from being crushed against the wall. Malevolent's eyes widened as he eased his grip on the piano.

"You're fucking finished!" Loco rammed the piano into Malevolent, causing him to hit his head against the cement wall. Malevolent collapsed on the floor, eyes shut, blood spewing from the side of his temple. It was over; he was on his way to meet Christ. He hoped his name was in the Book of Life: "Alejandro Valasquez." Also, he hoped to be reunited with his father. He wanted to forget all the chaos that occurred in his physical life and how things could have turned out for him.

Unfortunately, life hadn't turned out that way, and he probably felt he had let Portia down. Or maybe she believed he did the best he could.

Malevolent held a clenched fist, indicating he was in for the fight of his life. Loco's shadowy figure loomed over him as he lay on the floor, motionless. "I win! Portia's mine!" Loco searched his pockets but couldn't find the ruby ring. "Fuck!"

Then muffled radios, flashing lights, and the trampling feet of police officers stormed into the recording studio. "Hands up!" the boys in blue surrounded him, brandishing their firearms. Loco reached for a broken piano leg, charging at the officers. They opened fire, shooting him several times. Loco slumped to the floor, placing his hand on his chest and feeling the warm, bloody moisture. He took his last breath, closing his eyes. This sinister presence had taken Malevoent and Loco's life.

CHAPTER TWENTY-FIVE

On this gloomy morning, the weather was warm and windy, as if a thunderstorm was about to occur. If Malevolent witnessed his own funeral right now, he would agree with mother nature. Six pallbearers carried his black coffin, adorned with a bed of water-based spray-painted black roses, to the rear door of an open Cadillac hearse. Hundreds of his fans crowded the side-walks surrounding the Catholic church, tears streaming as they cheered, applauding a farewell to an artist gone too soon. The media, from local to national and international outlets, covered this sad event.

Then another six pallbearers carried a second black casket with Loco's body which was adorned with water-based spray-painted black roses, to another Cadillac hearse, sliding it in and shutting the door. The hip-hop duo's families, friends, and fellow rappers exited the church, crying, embracing one another, holding large photos and black roses. Erasmo and Martha hugged, crying and shaking their heads. Erasmo couldn't believe this was the same church where his son Edgar's funeral had been held. Now, it was for his grandson. He glanced over his shoulder, grabbing Aaron into his arms.

"I'm sorry. I could've done something," Aaron sobbed in Erasmo's embrace.

"There was nothing you could have done," Erasmo replied.

Rosa stood in the background, crying her eyes out. Aaron held his mother while Erasmo and Martha comforted her. Malevolent's aunts, Tatiana and Deborah, wore black dresses, looking older with salt-and-pepper hair and teary eyes as they embraced Aaron. Tatiana noticed Rosa standing right before her and embraced her. Deborah glared at her nephew's mother and turned away, still holding a grudge for what had occurred years earlier. And now, Rosa wasn't even in Alejandro's life, so why was she even there? Of course, Rosa's answer would be, "Alejandro's still my son!" she cried out.

Aaron consoled his mother, joined by other family members.

Seconds later, fans hurled black roses in the middle of the streets as the hearse carried Malevolent's body. Then fans tossed even more roses in the street as the second hearse hauling Loco's body made its way down the street. Fans cheered, applauded to this talented duo who will never be another. News reporters spoke to fans, capturing their opinions on this tragic event.

"Malevolent was so talented, and we lost him already," a female fan choked up as her friend hugged her.

"We can't believe this—MC Malevolent and DJ Loco dead over what?" a guy asked, shaking his head.

"A bitch!" said another guy in a stern tone.

"Don't say that!" the other members of the small group protested.

"What was she then? A groupie?"

"Our sources tell us that the woman in question is a classical pianist who added her talents to Malevolent's music," the news reporter responded.

"Think before you motherfucking speak, man!" the first guy hollered.

In a nearby Queens Park, two graffiti artists made the finishing touches of a mural of MC Malevolent and DJ Loco with black roses. Another group of fans came to witness the beautiful painting where they lit candles, laid artificial black roses, real roses, and prayed. The media covered the mural of the Hip-hop duo creation and spoke to fans who were to devastated and heartbroken to attend the funeral.

"This is unbelievable. Finally, we get some rap music that makes sense, makes you think, and groove. I'm sorry Hip-Hop is truly dead!" a girl cried as a guy embraced her.

"I'm sorry," the woman news reporter's voice quivered.

"It's not your fault! To tell you the truth, all music is dead!" the guy added.

Beaming spotlights lit up Radio City Music Hall; it was Grammy Night a year later. An enormous crowd of fans stood across the street, waiting to see their favorite music artists take their place on the red carpet. MC Malevolent and DJ Loco fans held black roses, large photos, and posters in their hands, hoping to see if these artists would be acknowledged for their contributions. Even though, this Hip-hop duo wasn't there physically, MC Malevolent and DJ Loco were there in spirit. The mass media, cameras, and photographers captured this glamorous yet emotional event. Private security, bodyguards, and the NYPD with K-9 units secured every angle of the theater. Fans took pictures and videos with their cellphones, attempting to catch a glimpse of their favorite rappers, singers, and bands.

Joey Jose and other NYC rappers swaggered along the red carpet with unpleasant expressions, dressed in black attire—whether streetwear or suits—holding black roses. A news reporter dashed to Joey Jose, shoving the microphone in his face. A guy from Joey's entourage yelled at her.

"Don't push me!" the news woman responded. "I just wanted to ask Joey a couple of questions!"

"Hurry and fucking ask!" Joe Jose stopped. The reporter smiled and put the microphone in his face. "How do you feel about your friends MC Malevolent and DJ Loco's passing?"

Joe and his entourage shook their heads, inhaling. "What do you think? That's a dumb question!"

"Okay. Was Malevolent and DJ Loco's fight over a woman?"

"No one knows," Joey Jose became irritated.

"If so, do you believe she was at fault?" the anchor woman pointed the microphone in his face.

“No! She wasn’t at fault. Shit happens, and when two men love a woman, they fight to the death. Thank you for your time!” Joe Jose and his entourage swaggered away. The news reporter gasped.

Well into the Grammy show, the audience applauded as two rappers stood at the podium to announce the Grammy award for the Best Hip-Hop Album of the Year. "And the Grammy goes to...," a popular rapper announced. Drum roll.

"Mourning Rose," MC Malevolent and DJ Loco. An enormous picture of the hip-hop duo displayed on the stage, with their music playing in the background. The audience applauded for the artists who fell short. Portia rose from her seat, dressed in a black evening gown with a white bow on the side, alongside Aaron (DJ Knucklehead), Benji, Joey Jose, and other artists as they escorted her to the stage. A standing ovation followed from the audience.

On behalf of Malevolent, DJ Loco, and their families, someone presented Portia with the Grammy, and she stepped up to the microphone. Feedback from the mic echoed throughout the auditorium.

“Sorry, everyone. Good evening, my name is Portia Fairchild. I'm the woman in the middle of this mess. I wish things had turned out differently. All I can say is that I love Alejandro Valasquez, aka C Malevolent. Malevolent, if you can hear me, I love you,” Portia wept as Joey Jose hugged her. There wasn't a dry eye in the audience. The world couldn't understand why Portia would expose herself like this. Some fans believed Portia was seeking attention and loved two men dying over her. Several individuals asserted that Malevolent and Loco's survival was contingent on Portia's actions, while others believed her side of the story.

Two years later, Portia glared at herself in a dressing room mirror with a dozen red roses that sat in a vase. She glared at the bright red floral and envisioned them being black because of her now tragic tale. Malevolent and Loco were gone and there's nothing she can do about it. She read the card on the vase of flowers that read: Have a great show, Aaron. Portia became watery eyed because he didn't blame her for the events that occurred. Some lives were lost or injured like Tony, the receptionist at the front desk was shot and got a second chance at life. Aaron's neighborhood friend, MC Chance, unfortunately didn't make it to see Hip-hop stardom. And several of Aaron's friends from the Lower East Side met their demise. Portia fortunately got a second chance as well to perform at the greatest concert hall which was Lincoln Center. Then there was a knock at the door as a stage manager peered his head in the dressing room. "Portia, you're up in five minutes."

"Okay, thank you," Portia nodded as she stood up, wearing a gorgeous black evening gown, primping her hair that was styled in a French roll with a side bang. She felt her hair was too plain, she grabbed two red roses from the vases, breaking off the long stems and put it in her hair. She took a deep breath, feeling beautiful and hoped that Malevolent could see her now. Portia sashayed to her dressing room door and opened as a bright light lit up her face automatically. She sensed as if she had gone to heaven to be reunited with Malevolent. She made her way across the enormous stage as an audience applauded. Portia didn't bother to look while she kept her focus on her performance. She sat at a black grand piano, placing her fingers on the keys and nodded at the orchestra. Seated a few feet away from her, Jazzy wearing a black dress, striking the bow on the strings of the cello. Jazzy took her cello lessons very seriously, going from groupie to professional celloist. At first, she envied Portia not only for her beauty, but true talents. Now, she's inspired by Portia's work. Portia proceeded to run her fingers along the keys as the symphony orchestra created a beautiful, somber tune. It was the classical version of "Roses Are Black."

THE END

ABOUT THE AUTHOR

Alexis Soleil is an American author from Flushing, New York, who writes dark/contemporary romances and literary fiction. She loses herself in her work while writing stories dealing with dangerous, forbidden romances with alpha males and traumatic tales involving family issues, etc. For fun, she loves going to museums, shopping, dining out, and travelling.

If you love a good dark romance with gritty, possessive characters that lean a little into the grey, you've come to the right place! Her earlier books such as "FROM THE OTHER SIDE OF THE TRACKS" and "IRATE" are great reads. And "Many Mansions," her third book, which is about fraternal twin brothers who take separate paths in life, is a great read. Her latest novel, "MALEVOLENT: A Hip-Hop Love Triangle," features shadowy undertones, danger, and alphas who fight for what they want in life.

Follow her www.tiktok.com/@alexissoleil

"Happy reading!"

www.ingramcontent.com/pod-product-compliance
Lightning Source LLC
LaVergne TN
LVHW090512110826
845146LV00003B/827

* 9 7 9 8 9 9 4 6 0 3 5 1 2 *